For Denise Little

Special thanks to Dr. Britta Reierson for answering all my questions.

CHAPTER ONE

"Your in-laws are scary," Phillipa Elliot told her sister, who made a lovely and not-in-the-least-blushing bride.

She leaned against the terrace railing next to Josephine and took another sip of very good champagne. The hot wind that blew in off the Las Vegas desert made her thirsty; she was probably on her fifth glass of champagne.

Jo's eyes went wide. "What do you mean by scary?"

Phillipa looked at the people dancing at the wedding reception in the hotel ballroom. "They make me feel like I've crashed the supermodels' annual ball."

Jo laughed. "Yeah, I know exactly what you mean." Her gaze didn't leave her new husband, who was currently dancing with their mother. "Isn't he —"

"Large," Phillipa cut in.

"I was going to say cute."

9

Phillipa laughed. "Of course you were."

The hulking groom was probably the *least* handsome man there, to her. Not that the muscular Marcus Cage didn't have enough charm and charisma for three normal males. It seemed to run in the Cage family, and among all their friends. The women were amazingly beautiful, mostly in a dark and mysterious way. And the men — good lord!

They'd been hitting on her since the rehearsal dinner the night before. It was quite a stimulating experience.

Phillipa fanned her face. She wasn't sure if it was the champagne or the mere thought of the men at the reception that was causing the warmth that stirred through her. There was something special about this bunch. As a cop, she was used to working around hunky, hard-bodied, macho men, and liked it. But the Cages and their friends had so much going for them in the confident, sexy male department that they were downright daunting.

"It's not that I don't like the Cage clan," Phillipa explained.

"Family," Josephine said. "They're a family, not a clan."

"What difference does that make?"

Jo laughed. "Never mind, and I can't explain anyway. If I did, they'd probably have to kill you. It's a joke," she added quickly. "Between Marc and me."

Phillipa let it go. Far be it from her to try to interpret the private language of newly-wed lovebirds, especially after five glasses of champagne.

She looked at her empty glass and said, "I'm switching to water." One of the groom's hunky relatives was headed their way, his gaze fixed on her. "Now," she added, and left so he'd have to ask her sister to dance instead of her.

The band stopped playing as she skirted the dance floor, and she noticed Marc heading for Jo and Mom heading toward where Dad waited for her. Phillipa smiled, appreciating the devotion of the happy couples — though she had to fight off a twinge of sadness at being alone herself. She blamed the self-pity on the champagne; she had no one to blame for breaking up with Patrick but Patrick. You'd think with all the gorgeous men in the place, she thought, I'd be more interested than daunted by the prospect of hooking up with one of them.

Maybe I don't want another macho man. Maybe that was why all the groom's male relatives set off alarm bells she couldn't explain.

The band started playing again as she

reached the bar.

"Not more Queen," a man said behind her.

The disgust in his voice amused her, and the deep British accent was intriguing. As the band played "Another One Bites the Dust," she took the water the bartender handed her, then turned around. She hadn't seen the man standing behind her before, though she was somehow already aware of his presence before he spoke. His hair was wavy and sandy brown, his eyes green and surrounded by laugh lines. He had a lived-in face; a dangerous face.

"I know what you mean," she told him. "If they play 'Fat Bottomed Girls,' I'm out of here."

"I'll join you," he answered.

"And, if they play a lot of Def Leppard, Jo will probably run away screaming."

The newcomer followed Phillipa as she edged around the dance floor toward the terrace.

"Who's Jo, and what's wrong with Def Leppard? I'm a proud son of Sheffield myself," he added. "Same hometown as the Lep—"

"Wait. What do you mean, *who's Jo?*" Phillipa stopped and confronted him. "You *are* a guest at the Elliot-Cage wedding, aren't you?"

His smile was devastating, showing deep dimples and crinkling the lines around his eyes. "I'm the best man."

Irritation flared over the heat that had been roused by his smile. "You're Matt Bridger! You very nearly ruined this wedding!" she accused.

"It's not my fault my plane was late."

"You were supposed to have arrived yesterday."

He gestured at the boisterous people filling the crowded room. "It doesn't look like I was missed."

"One of my brothers stepped in as best man."

"Then it all turned out all right." He crossed his arms over his wide chest and moved close to her. "I don't know what you have to be angry about."

"I'm angry on my sister's behalf."

"Why's that?"

"She's Jo Elliot."

"The singer in Def Leppard?"

"The bride!"

Even as she indignantly stepped closer, Phillipa realized that Matt Bridger was teasing her.

Suddenly they were toe to toe and nose to nose. He put an arm around her waist,

13

drawing her even closer. She was caught by the masculine heat and scent of him. "You're provoking me on purpose."

The back of his hand brushed across her cheek. "Yes."

Her knees went weak, and she almost dropped her glass. She didn't notice where it went when he took it out of her hand.

"Dance with me."

"Yes."

Of course. She never wanted to dance with anyone else.

He drew her onto the dance floor, and they started slow-dancing to the fast music. It was the most natural thing in the world to gaze into this stranger's eyes and press her body against his, soft and hard blending. They didn't share a word while the music played, yet the communication between them was deep and profound. She'd known him forever, been waiting for him forever. It was all too perfect to make any sense.

When the music stopped she would've kept right on dancing, but Matt Bridger turned them off the dance floor. Her arms stayed draped around his wide shoulders, and her gaze stayed locked on his. His palms pressed against the small of her back, large and warm and possessive.

Despite this intimate closeness, Phillipa tried to regain her sanity.

"We've just met."

"And you're really not that kind of girl."

"What kind of girl?"

"The sort who snuggles up to a stranger the moment they meet. And I'm not that sort of man." He flashed that devastating smile at her again. "Mostly."

"Then why are you and I —"

"We have more than snuggling in mind."

"Yes, but —"

"I have a theory."

She didn't want to hear his theory. "Kiss me."

Fingers traced across her lips. "Soon."

His touch left her sizzling. This was crazy! She should be embarrassed.

She took a deep breath, and made an effort to step away. She managed to move maybe an inch, making it a small triumph for public decency.

"Like calls to like," he said, pulling her back to him.

She lost interest in decency. "I'm a cop."

"Fancy that." As the music started again, he took her by the hand. The connection was electric. "Come on."

She held back. This was her last chance to stay virtuous. "I don't —"

"Listen."

She did, and laughed. "Oh, my God, 'Fat Bottomed Girls.' "

"You said you'd leave if they played it."

"Left alone with big fat Fanny —"

"Matt Bridger, let's get out of here."

They headed toward the door, but he stopped after a few steps. "One thing, first."

"What?"

"Your name."

"Phillipa Elliot."

Now, at least, she wasn't about to fall into reckless abandon with a *total* stranger.

He tilted his head and gave her a quick, thorough once-over. What he saw was a tall blond woman in a strapless, tea-length teal satin bridesmaid's dress.

"I know, I don't look like a Phillipa," she said. "But who does?"

"Pardon me for saying so, but that is an unfortunate name for a Yank, isn't it?"

"I'm used to it."

"Good. It suits you."

The band started to play louder, and they ran for the door.

They kissed in the elevator, coming together in a rush of heat. His mouth was hard and demanding on hers, and she responded just as fiercely. He caressed her in a way that

16

made her feel naked despite the satin dress and layers of underwear. His fingers tracing along her bare shoulders and the back of her neck drove her wild. She knew this was crazy, but she didn't care.

Until she noticed that her skirt was hiked up around one hip, and his hand was stroking the inside of her thigh. It felt wonderful.

"We're not exactly private here," she reminded him. "Hotel" — she gasped as his fingers moved higher — "security."

"Room key," was his answer.

He stopped long enough for her to fumble open her tiny purse, and the doors slid open onto the fourteenth floor just as she pulled out the black plastic key card.

"This is it." She gave him a sideways glance. "I wonder which one of us remembered to press the button for the right floor."

She thought he had, but it must have been her, since she was sure she hadn't told him where her room was.

The room wasn't far from the elevators, and they were inside within a few moments.

A few moments after that, he'd whirled her around and onto the bed.

"You make me dizzy," she said as he leaned over her and she looked into his green eyes.

"Only dizzy?"

There was a wicked glint in those eyes, and a world of sensual promise in his slight smile. There was also something dangerous about his deep, slightly rough voice. The sound of it sent a thrill through her.

"Say something else."

He chuckled. "What is it about Yank women and English accents?"

"Don't complain if it helps you get laid," she told him.

He laughed again. "Would this sound seductive in Sheffield?" he asked, doing a very good job of mimicking an American accent.

"Yes. But it's not just your accent that's sexy. You have gorgeous lips," she added. When she traced them with a finger, he nipped it. "And sharp teeth."

"Oh, yes." He kissed her throat.

Her blood raced as warm lips pressed against her tender skin. His hand brushed across the satin covering her breast, sparking an overwhelming desire to have his naked flesh against hers.

A moment later he tugged her to her feet and pulled down the dress's long zipper. As the dress pooled around her feet, his thumb slid slowly down the length of her bare spine. She arched against him.

"Skin on skin, just like you want," he

murmured. His lips were close to her ear. Then they were on her throat.

There was a moment of sharp pain, followed by blinding ecstasy. When her mind cleared from the blissful overload, they were back on the bed once more, and he was as naked as she was. She ran her hands across his chest, appreciating the sight and texture of hard muscles and hot flesh.

"You are so sweet," he told her.

"I'm more than sweet." She pulled his head down and kissed him hard.

"You're also hot," he agreed.

He kissed her gently on the lips, on the cheek, but she was aware of the edge of ferocity he was holding back. Then his head moved down and his tongue swirled around one hard nipple, then the other.

She moaned, and inside the needy sound she heard his voice. *I'm trying to stay civilized.*

Don't, she answered.

His touch grew rougher then, and her responses were just as frantic. He kissed and bit her all over. Each pinprick of pain that followed the soft brush of lips across her skin brought her a flash of mounting pleasure.

The contrast was maddening. Wonderful.

With each flash, the heat pooling in her belly grew and spread until the orgasms became one long, continuous wave of ecstasy. She didn't think it could get better, until he was inside her, filling her with hard, fast strokes that drowned her in fiery sensation. She clung to him, rose to meet him with the same manic energy, wanted nothing but more.

And more was what he gave her. She gave herself up to him, blended with him, blood, mind, and soul, and he gave himself to her. She was complete with him, whole with him, in nirvana, until one last, shattering explosion sent her over the edge and into darkness.

"That was —" Phillipa sighed, unable to describe the experience. Now she understood why sex was called "the little death." Maybe it was just *great* sex that was called that.

Little sparks of pleasure were still shooting through her; she was exhilarated and exhausted at the same time. She was completely content to lie across Matt, her breasts pressed against the hard muscles of his bare chest. She rested her cheek against the warmth of his skin and breathed in the male scent of him.

"It certainly was," Matt answered.

She glanced up to see his hands propped

behind his head, a smug smile curving his beautiful mouth. She caught the sparkle of green in his half-closed eyes.

"You look like a well-fed cat," she told him.

"Very well-fed," he answered. "But still hungry."

He pulled her up the length of his body for a kiss. His mouth was as insistent and needy as if they hadn't just made love. He made her hungry all over again. His hands began to roam, and her body responded.

This time she was able to keep her head long enough to say, "Maybe we shouldn't." His mouth circled a nipple. "Oh God! I mean — there's supposed to be photos — and — wedding stuff." Her mind was too into the pleasure to remember just what. "We'll be missed."

He nuzzled her, and his voice came muffled from between her breasts. "Do you really care?"

"Nooo — yes! We'll be missed. I should be there. She's my sis—" She suddenly became very aware of his erection, and her hand closed around it. She *had* to touch him, to stroke him. "I shouldn't be doing this."

"You better not stop."

His hungry growl sent a needy shiver

through her. His voice was enough to make her melt. "But —"

This sort of thing happens at family gatherings all the time.

"What happens?"

People disappear to make love. It's a way to celebrate the bonding.

"That's nice." It occurred to Phillipa that there was something odd about this conversation. "Did you just say something inside my head?"

Not that you'll recall. Relax, sweetness. Make love to me.

"All right." It was all she wanted to do anyway.

As a carousel version of "Ode to Joy" woke Phillipa, she thought, I belong with this man. When she came a further awake, she realized that the noise was a cell phone ringing, and that she was lying naked in a dark hotel room with Matt Bridger. She couldn't think of anywhere better to be, and snuggled closer to him while Beethoven kept playing.

Eventually Matt rolled over and picked the phone up from the nightstand. "Mike, if you're drunk, you're a dead lobo."

Whatever the answer was, it made Matt sit up. His muscles bunched with tension. "Where and when? Right. I'm not alone."

Deciding to let him ride out this emergency in privacy, Phillipa slid out of bed and crossed the dark room to the bathroom. There she took her time using the facilities and drinking a glass of water.

Even as she stepped back into the bedroom, she was aware of the emptiness. The musky tang of sex was still in the air, but even before she turned on a light and saw the rumpled, empty bed, she knew he was gone.

CHAPTER TWO

Three years later

If there was one thing Phillipa didn't like about hotel bathrooms, it was that the shower was always directly across from the mirror. Even with the glass all steamed up, she could see herself when she stepped out. She knew that, at least on the outside, she had a perfectly good body. The scar on her arm didn't bother her.

But she didn't like seeing the splotchy line of fading and fresh bruises across the flat expanse of her stomach. She made herself look, because one couldn't be a coward about these things. She made herself think about how pretty the small black and gold sun symbol she'd recently had inked onto her stomach was. It was the one area where she never stuck the needle.

Deciding she was being maudlin, she grabbed a towel and dried off quickly. Her sister was waiting, and it had been months since they'd seen each other. She dressed in shorts and a tank top, then went into the bedroom.

Of course the first thing Jo did was ask, "How's your arm? Does it hurt?"

I should have worn sleeves. "I hardly notice it." Phillipa touched the scar and gave a faint laugh. "Getting shot's what saved my life, you know." It was true, even if she did resent it, even though she knew that was stupid. She sat on the bed, since Jo had the room's one chair. She glanced out the wide window that looked out on the Las Vegas strip. The Bellagio's huge fountain danced in the distance. "The view's gorgeous from up here. Even in the daylight."

"You know you could have stayed at our place," Jo answered.

"Uh-uh." Phillipa counted off on her fingers. "You have a new baby, a mother-in-law, and a grandmother-in-law staying at your place. I'm not going near that mix."

"I see your point." Jo grinned.

"And didn't you bring young Brandon Matthias Cage here with you?" *Is Matt short for Matthias? And why am I thinking about him? Because I'm in a hotel room in Vegas?* She waved an admonitory finger at her younger sister. "Where's my nephew?"

"He's safe at home, surrounded by overprotective Cage women. And I am getting a little antsy about it."

"Says the equally overprotective new mother."

"I'm new at this mom thing. I like it," Jo added.

"Which means you want to get home soon so you can get back to it. You didn't have to meet me here."

"I was told I needed a break, and there's no way Marc was going to let me help with the party. Besides, I wanted a chance to talk to you alone."

"Having a husband that's a better cook than you must be great," Phillipa said.

"I love it. I fly planes, he caters parties; it works for us. Not that I plan to fly much until Brandon's older."

"You're giving up piloting? Does Dad know about this?"

Jo laughed. "He's a granddad now, which makes him all for my staying on the ground with his infant grandson. Which leaves an opening at Elliot Charter — at least, a temporary one."

Phillipa got the hint. "Sorry, I'm a cop."

"You can fly a plane."

"I don't have the rating to do it professionally, and I might not qualify. Besides, I like what I do."

"But —"

"Vegas hotels are always looking for good security people. I thought I'd look into it while I'm here." She was still officially on the force even if she wasn't on active duty. She didn't know if she'd ever get back on the streets. "I have to think about my future, even if all I want is to get back what I had."

Damn! She'd vowed not to whine about anything!

Jo, of course, ran with it. "How are you feeling?"

The look of concern on her sister's face bruised Phillipa.

"I'm fine."

It was an easier answer than explaining about how there were good days and bad days, and how sometimes she was nauseated, and sometimes her vision was blurry, and she was always cold, and she wanted everything to go back to normal — but she was stuck with a life that was regulated, constricted, and she didn't know who she was anymore.

"You're not," Jo answered. "I'm an empath, remember?"

Jo did have this gift for reading peoples' emotions. Phillipa had a variation of it herself, though not as strong. She trusted her instincts when it came to telling the

27

good guys from the bad guys. The ability to read people had saved her ass on the street a few times.

"I don't feel fine," she admitted to her sister. "I feel — complicated. But healthier," she added, trying to project sincerity.

Her cell phone rang before Jo could press for more details. By the time she was finished with a short conversation, Jo was using her own cell.

"Party crisis?" Phillipa asked when Jo was done.

"Yep. Marc's mom is frantic, but he says it's under control."

"It?"

"Something about meringue swans breaking and flowers that were delivered to the restaurant instead of the house. As long as the baby is fine, I don't care."

"Is the baby fine?"

"I'm still here, aren't I? Who were *you* talking to?"

"Little sisters shouldn't be so nosy."

"It sounded like it had to do with your love life."

"You should definitely stop being nosy. But since I invited him to your party, I'll let you get away with it this time," Phillipa teased.

"Him?"

"A friend. An LVPD detective."

"A hunky friend?" Jo prodded.

Phillipa nodded.

"I look forward to meeting him."

"He called to tell me he can't make it tonight. He says there's been a rash of robberies that has everybody pulling extra shifts."

"Oh, yeah, I heard about it on the news. Banks and some of the smaller casinos have been hit." Jo stood up. "Listen, I know we said we were going to do lunch, but —"

"But the antsy new mom wants to go home to her kid."

Jo gave a sheepish smile. "Yeah."

Phillipa waved toward the door. "Then you should go."

"You could come with."

Phillipa shook her head. "I'll coo and fuss over him tonight. You go home, and I'll finish unpacking and making phone calls and stuff."

"You're sure?"

"I'm sure. Go."

"You'll be all right by yourself?"

"Go mother Brandon, not me. Go," Phillipa repeated.

Jo left after a quick hug and kiss.

Phillipa sighed with relief. It wasn't that she couldn't have made it through an afternoon and evening of socializing, but now she didn't have to. Now she could take a nap.

"You're late."

"You're lucky I came at all," Michele answered the vampire. "And I don't appreciate being searched. I don't carry weapons to public places."

"Weapons that harm humans, you mean," the vampire said. "But my man outside did relieve you of a pair of silver bracelets. Those could be used as weapons against my kind. I think I have a right to a certain amount of paranoia when negotiating with a Purist."

Michele shrugged.

When the vampire gestured toward a chair, Michele hesitated a moment before taking a seat. "It's more contempt than paranoia on my part," she explained.

"But neither of us wants to appear conspicuous out here" — the vampire cast a significant look around the room packed with crowded tables — "among all these innocent civilians."

Michele Darabont did not want to be in the same room with a vampire, let alone sitting across a restaurant table from one, but one did what one had to for the Cause. She took a seat.

"Was that a threat?" she asked.

"Oh, please. Let's cut the melodrama crap, shall we?"

"You started it." God, she sounded like a fool!

"And you are thinking that this petulance is no way for an experienced hunter to behave. It was a long drive from San Diego to Las Vegas, you're tired, and you think I'm supercilious. No, I'm not reading your mind; I can read your expression well enough. Let's start over, shall we? Can I call you Michele?"

"No."

"No introductions, then. Let's think of each other as the Purist and the monster."

"I'm not a Purist. No Purist would have a face-to-face with one of your kind. I have worked with your sort before."

Which was why several of her friends who were members of the Purist cult had persuaded her to represent them at this meeting, after the vampire's message mysteriously arrived. The Purist agenda was to kill the ancient enemy before asking questions, but they were intrigued enough by this proposal to want to explore the possibilities, even if they wouldn't do it themselves.

"I don't blame you for not liking to work

31

with *my sort.*" A waiter approached, and the vampire waited until he'd left with Michele's order for iced tea before going on. "I, on the other hand, am neutral about *your sort.* I've never killed a human, and my blood sources are all volunteers. This is the twenty-first century. It's better to share the world than to make war on each other."

Michele did not agree with this live-and-let-live philosophy, but most vampire hunters did. All but the Purists. While she hadn't quite stepped over the line that divided the hunter camps, she'd always been close to it. She'd recently discovered that her niece Eden had betrayed the hunter's beliefs, which was causing Michele to edge closer to the extremists' views.

"Why do you want to help the Purists?" she asked.

The vampire laughed. "I *am* a purist."

The waiter arrived with her tea, so all Michele could do was stare incredulously at the beautiful creature across the table until he was gone. Then she said, "I don't understand."

"I believe in the purity of my own kind, just as you believe in the purity of yours. I want to help my own species. While I do believe in most of the covenants of the hunter and vampire truce, there is one function you humans once performed that helped keep the vampire race from becoming tainted and weak.

"There are those among us who wish a return to that ancient practice. We are as much a minority among vampires as the Purists are among the human hunters. In this one thing we are in agreement. In this one thing, we can join forces."

"You're talking about the Abominations."

The vampire looked disgusted. "There are those who prefer terms like niece, nephew, grandson, and so on, but I am not one who believes that the offspring of our mating with humans should be considered family. Thanks to centuries of being hunted by your kind, our pure population is low enough that our people are forced to mate with yours."

"It's *our* fault that your damn Primes seduce girls away to —"

The vampire held up a hand to cut her off. "Oh, please. I know all about how your niece ran off with one of our boys. You have my sympathy, and every reason to be indignant, but Eden went with Laurent of her own free will. It happens. Live with it. I have to live with similar situations in my own family.

"What should *not* happen is reproduction

between your kind and mine. Hunters used to be very good at culling the mules born into the Clans and Families, and the Tribes were wise enough to take care of the problem on their own. These days we are all too civilized, too domesticated to take the necessary measures. The breeding has to stop." The vampire turned a dark, compelling stare on her. "Don't you agree?"

Michele could not look away. The world slowed down, and reality shifted. She'd been trained to resist vampire tricks, but all she could do was say, "What do you want me to do?"

CHAPTER THREE

"Showtime," Phillipa murmured as the elevator came to a stop.

She'd had a nap, used the hotel fitness center, and done some shopping before heading for Jo's condo for the prechristening party. She felt refreshed, and even if she wasn't in the mood for a party, she was looking forward to spending some time with her brand-new nephew. Assuming she could get past the Cage relatives to do it.

They're good people, she told herself. Loving and loyal — and loud. Very East Coast, very urban and in-your-face. Very — whatever their ethnicity is.

Phillipa hesitated when the copper-plated doors of the elevator slid open. Maybe she'd just been focused on herself too much lately, too much inside her own head. Or maybe she hesitated because the last time she'd been at a party with the Cages, she'd made a fool of herself.

That was different. He won't be here.

She stepped into the hallway and walked with firm steps toward her sister's door.

Jo and Marcus were not full-time residents of Las Vegas; they lived in New York a good part of the year and kept a condo in a Vegas high-rise for the rest of the year. Phillipa thought of her hulking brother-in-law as more of a Marine DI type than a celebrity chef and restaurateur, but he loved cooking.

The door opened before she could ring the bell, and Marcus Cage filled the doorway. "You're going to love what I made for you," he announced in his deep, growly voice, and swept her into a hug and into the condo. "You've lost weight," he said once he let her go.

"I got shot."

"You're all muscle, though," He ran his hands up her arms and down her waist. "Skinny, but choice. Kind of like Josephine when I met her. But ticklish," he added when she squirmed under his touch. He held her out at arm's length. "How are you feeling?"

"I get asked that a lot. Where's my nephew?"

"Come with me."

He led her into a huge living room where a wide expanse of windows overlooked the brightly lit city below. The view of Las Vegas at night was dizzying, so Phillipa concentrated on the dozen people gathered on couches and chairs in the center of the room. The men all stood when she entered, a very old-world and polite thing to do. The women always looked like they were waiting to have their hands kissed. Phillipa hadn't been around the in-laws enough to get used to it, but Jo seemed comfortable with their ways.

Better her than me. Phillipa told herself it was her imagination that she received a couple of sharp looks for her thought.

Jo was seated on the central couch, holding Brandon on her lap. Phillipa smiled with pleasure at the sight of the baby, and with pride when she noticed that her nephew was wrapped in the white baby blanket that she'd knitted for him.

"Mom called," Jo said as Phillipa approached. "Guess whose flight was delayed? She'll be staying in Newark tonight, so she and Dad will be in tomorrow. Dad's been making the usual disparaging comments about her flying commercial, and she has pointed out that she's aware of the irony of the situation."

"This leaves you with a heavy burden of responsibility," Marc said, putting his arm around Phillipa's shoulders. "Since your brothers' reserve units were called up."

Her brothers were military police pilots, as she was — had been — military police. And her National Guard unit was on active duty, as well. She hated the reminder of one more part of her life she was missing.

"And what would that responsibility be?" she asked.

"Representing the entire Elliot family at this party, of course. That means you'll have to eat for all of them."

"I'm on a very strict diet," she reminded her brother-in-law. "You'll have to live with leftovers."

She sat down next to her sister and held her arms out. "Give me the kid."

The doorbell rang, and Marc went to answer it. Phillipa had the impression of the Cage women tensing when Jo handed the baby to her. All those dark-eyed women watched her like hawks as she settled the small, warm bundle in her lap.

"He is, of course, gorgeous and perfect, in the way of his kind," she said.

"What do you mean, his kind?" his paternal grandmother asked.

Phillipa laughed, hoping to dispel the odd tension. "He's gorgeous and perfect in the way all newborns seem to their mothers and other relatives."

Grandma Cage relaxed and smiled. "Ah. Yes."

Peering closer at the tiny perfection of Brandon Cage's features, Phillipa said, "Jo, do you know that he already has a tooth? Babies don't come with teeth, do they?"

"He came that way," Jo answered.

"It's natural — for *our* kind," a great-aunt spoke up.

"Octavia," Grandma Cage said warningly.

"Marc tells me that early dental development runs in the Cage family," Jo said. "It's a genetic thing."

Phillipa frequently got the impression that whenever she found out anything about the Cages, the information was a little skewed. Her intuition told her that the family used the truth to obscure even deeper truths.

"What's a genetic thing?" Marc asked, coming back into the room with four more guests.

"Nothing," Jo answered. She stood up for greetings and hugs. Once she'd seen Brandon safely into the arms of another cooing woman, Jo said to her husband, "You want me to help you in the kitchen."

Marc took this hint that his wife wanted a private conversation.

"When do we eat?" Phillipa asked as they

headed, arm in arm, out of the room.

Marc glanced back. "Ten minutes."

Phillipa excused herself and headed for the guest bathroom, which was across the hall from the kitchen. Once she'd shot up and tucked her equipment back into her large purse, she stepped back into the hall.

As she returned to the living room, she paused when she heard Jo say, "I still don't like the idea of my sister not remembering the whole event."

"She'll remember," Marc said reassuringly. "Just not necessarily the way it actually happens."

"Why are you comfortable with that?"

"Honey, you know that's the way we have to live."

"She thinks she's going to be Brandon's godmother."

"She will be — in a way."

Phillipa was so surprised by this odd conversation that she was tempted to barge into the kitchen and demand to know what the hell was going on, but she doubted that was the easiest way to get at the truth.

"I understand the need for discretion, but —"

"In the old days, our bondmates had to sever all ties with their own kind."

This was as confusing as it was disturbing. She didn't handle confusion well at the moment. What she craved was simple, solid routine. Phillipa rubbed a hand across her eyes. She was a little dizzy. And since her head was not on too straight at the moment, maybe all this ominous-sounding stuff wasn't ominous at all.

"These days we're more accommodating," he went on, "but there are rules. They're for everyone's protection. You agreed to the rules."

"I know, but —"

"Josephine."

"All right, all right. You don't have to take that lord and master tone with me, Marcus Cage."

He answered with a deep, rumbling laugh. The solid, normal sound blew away some of Phillipa's confusion. Jo laughed as well, a throaty, sexy sound Phillipa wasn't used to coming from her little sister. After that there was a lengthy silence, which Phillipa interpreted as a happily married couple making out in their kitchen. That was sweet and all, but what had they been talking about?

And, even more important, would their snogging delay dinner? She had to eat within half an hour of shooting up. A confrontation might be necessary, to get closer to the food.

41

But before she could enter the kitchen Jo and Marc came out, their arms around each other's waists. Jo looked surprised to see her.

Phillipa refused to be embarrassed at being in the hall. She looked at her watch, then significantly at Marc. "You said ten minutes."

"You're a slave to your stomach," Marc said. "I like that in a woman." He held Jo tighter. "When Josephine was pregnant, she appreciated my skills."

"I ate like a horse."

"Now she's back to skin and bones and no appetite."

"He means that now I eat like a small horse."

"Come along, you two."

Marc turned Jo around, and they headed back into the kitchen. Phillipa followed, and was put to work helping to carry plates and platters and bowls into the dining room. Everything looked and smelled delicious.

"Even if I wasn't a slave to carbohydrate exchanges, this feast would make me hungry," she told Marc when they stood back to look upon the laden table. She popped a pepperoncini into her mouth and sighed at the crisp heat of the pickled pepper.

"You have a fondness for hot things."

There was a wicked gleam in Marc's dark eyes as he put his arm around her shoulders. "And I just had a great idea."

"What's that?" Phillipa asked, and speared a mushroom with a toothpick. "Spicy," she added when she bit into it.

"Spicy is what you need." He gave a deep, dirty chortle. "What you need, Elliot, is a vampire."

She gave Marc a puzzled look. "I do not get this joke."

"I'm serious. What's wrong with you boils down to a serious blood disorder, right?"

"Not exact—"

"If you share blood with a vampire, that'll cure it."

"That's an interesting theory," she answered. "But it has a slight flaw in it."

"Vampires are very sexy," he told her. "You'd enjoy the cure."

"I'm sure I would. Except for the fact that there's no such thing as vampires."

He cocked an eyebrow. "You sure?"

"Not in the reality I live in."

"I'll introduce you to one from mine."

Phillipa edged away from her brother-in-law. "Okay, Marc. You find me a vampire, and I'll let him bite me."

"Deal," he said with a grin.

"What are you up to, Marc?" Jo asked,

coming into the dining room.

"Oh, nothing."

Jo narrowed her eyes at the false innocence of his answer. "Did I hear a *bad* word just now?"

"You know I never swear."

"You know what I mean."

"I don't," Phillipa spoke up.

The doorbell rang before she got an answer, and Marc hastily left the room.

"It's kind of cute, seeing a big man look that sheepish," Jo said, gazing fondly after her husband. She followed after him.

Phillipa gazed fondly at the feast spread out on the table, then followed her sister toward the front door. Feeling curiouser and curiouser, she intended to find out what these two were talking about.

But she stopped dead in her tracks when she heard a familiar British voice say, "I said I'd be your eldest child's guardian, but I thought I'd have a few more decades before I'd have to make good on the promise."

Her insides curled, and her heart raced.

Good God, what's he doing here?

Her first impulse was to hide, but it was already too late. All she could do was try not to look stunned as Jo and Marc came back down the hallway, Matt Bridger walking between them.

44

CHAPTER FOUR

Phillipa forced a smile. "Nice to see you again, Matt."

Jo said, "I forgot you two knew each other."

"I didn't," Marc said.

"Hello," Bridger said, stopping in front of her.

Too close. He smiled, and everything inside her went *zing*. It was totally unfair of her body to respond this way three years after a one-night stand, for goodness sake!

She took a step back, only to have him follow. He put his hand on her shoulder, and fire went all the way through her.

She saw the fire reflected in his eyes and thought, Oh, no, it's starting all over again! She tried to move away, but moved closer to him instead.

Jo came forward and took Matt by the arm. "Let's introduce you to the family."

Matt's gaze didn't leave Phillipa's. "I've

already met the family."

"Time to get reacquainted," Jo persisted, and tugged him forward.

Matt threw a hard look at Marc over his shoulder as he was led away.

Then Marc gallantly offered Phillipa his arm.

"Now that both godparents have arrived, the party can finally get started. The fireworks already have."

"What?"

"You two are our guests of honor," he said. "You're going to have a lovely evening."

"I'd rather leave," she told her brother-in-law.

"Oh, no, there's no escaping it. Trust me, I know."

"As usual, I don't know what you're talking about."

"You'll find out soon enough. Dinner!" the deep-voiced Marc announced as they entered the living room.

"A toast!"

Oh, lord, not another one, Phillipa thought, but dutifully lifted her glass of water as one of Marc's male relatives rose to his feet.

Matt was seated across the table next to Octavia, who was blatantly flirting with him.

He didn't seem to mind, and Phillipa was glad he was being distracted. *Really.*

But he'd seemed interested in her when he walked in, so how come he was ignoring her now?

Probably because Octavia was vivacious and gorgeous, and obviously available. Phillipa got the impression they already knew each other in a biblical fashion. Which made Bridger something of a slut. Which was none of her business, but didn't say much for her taste in men.

And why should she care if he ignored her? Because her own date hadn't been able to make it tonight? Which she hadn't minded until Bridger walked in.

He leaned forward now and asked, "Don't you drink wine?"

Phillipa was so surprised that her glass slipped out of her hand.

Bridger plucked it out of the air before she even saw him move. He smiled.

Her heart turned over, and she forgot to breathe.

"The last time we met," he said, "you tasted of champagne."

His words had no business feeling like a caress, yet memories registered on her skin.

"To Matthias and Phillipa, the child's guardians!" the man giving the toast exclaimed.

She was aware that everyone's gaze was now on her, but Phillipa could only look into Matt Bridger's eyes. The connection was still there, stronger, even after three years.

She dimly heard applause.

Then Bridger said, "We're supposed to bow to the parents of our goddess child now."

"Not to follow our custom would be rude, mort-miss," Octavia added.

Phillipa managed to drag her attention to the other woman. She had her hand possessively on Bridger's arm. She didn't look at all happy that he was talking to Phillipa.

"We wouldn't want to be rude," he said. "Come, Phillipa." He stood.

So did she, and it felt as if she was drawn to her feet by the force of his will. This is distinctly not normal, she thought.

"Like so," he said, and bowed from the waist.

After all the years she'd studied martial arts, she had plenty of practice at this. She bowed politely to Jo and Marc, and this signaled the end of the meal. Most of the guests headed toward the living room. Octavia put her arm through Matt's and led him away. Phillipa stayed to help clean off the table.

She took a stack of plates into the kitchen, and Jo pounced as soon as the door closed behind her.

"So, you know Matt?"

Phillipa didn't like her sister's suspicious tone. "We're not exactly friends," she answered as she set the plates on the counter next to the sink. "I don't know him — except in the biblical sense," she admitted at Jo's withering look.

"So I gathered." She put her hands on her hips. "When?"

"At your wedding reception."

"I didn't know he made it to the wedding."

"I'm told brides don't remember much about the wedding. He was there. Briefly. Then he and I — sort of had a brief encounter."

"Sort of? How brief?"

Phillipa winced. "Okay, we fucked like bunnies."

"Oh, good lord, no." Jo pressed a hand to her forehead, then touched the side of her throat. "Please tell me he didn't — do anything kinky."

"That's none of your business. Besides, being grilled on my sex life by my little sister is not my idea of a good time."

"I don't have to be a good hostess with you." She turned very serious, very concerned. "You can't get involved with someone like Matt Bridger, hon."

"I'm not involv—"

"You've been radiating lust ever since he arrived."

"That's not —"

"He's a very dangerous man."

Phillipa bridled. "I'm a dangerous woman."

"Not at the moment, you're not. You're — vulnerable — right now. You couldn't handle someone like him." She put her hands on Phillipa's shoulders. "Promise me you'll stay away from him. Besides, aren't you seeing a local cop?"

"Not exactly seeing." She sighed. She couldn't be angry at her sister's concern; she was glad of the reminder. "We're friends — with potential. He's nice, normal. I doubt Matt Bridger is either one."

"You can say that again."

"But Bridger makes me feel all unfocused and fuzzy — and hot."

"Like champagne zinging through your bloodstream."

Exactly. Phillipa eyed her sister suspiciously. "How'd you know about that?"

Jo laughed. "I've made love to Marc a few

times. The males of his family are intoxicating."

Phillipa stepped away from Jo's gentle grasp. "I don't need to be intoxicated right now." She glanced toward the kitchen door. "Besides, Octavia's reminding Bridger of their old acquaintance at the moment. She's welcome to him."

Something primal deep inside Phillipa growled with jealousy, though, and the strong feeling scared her. "I just don't want to watch the seduction, and I'm getting pretty tired anyway," she told her sister. "Is it okay with you if I kiss my peacefully sleeping nephew good night, then head back to the hotel?"

"I think that might be for the best," Jo said. "If I'm lucky I can get everybody to leave soon." She gave a slow, sexy smile. "I'm in the mood for some champagne myself tonight."

What had Jo meant about Bridger being dangerous? The question didn't occur to Phillipa until she was in the elevator. Oh, she recognized a predator when she saw one, and Bridger was definitely one of her own kind. But what did her gentle little sister know about the man? Why was Jo so worried about her hooking up with him?

She was tempted to go back and ask her sister what she meant.

"Tomorrow," she told her reflection in the copper-plated doors. She'd ask Jo when she saw her at the church tomorrow. Of course, Bridger would be there as well, but a christening ceremony was hardly the setting for lust and seduction.

And let us not forget Octavia, and her designs on Mr. Bridger's fine, fine physique, she thought as the elevator opened on the lobby. I'll try to think chaste thoughts tomorrow. And think of Octavia as my guardian angel.

She exited the building, and all chaste intentions left her as soon as she spotted Matt leaning against her car in the well-lit visitor's parking lot.

"What are you doing here?" she demanded.

His gaze went over her with the same heat and intensity it had had when they'd met earlier. "I want a ride."

"Try Octavia," was her instant, angry response.

He chuckled. "I don't normally find jealousy attractive in a woman, but you wear it well."

She barely caught herself from snapping that she wasn't jealous, which would have sounded childish and stupid.

"I want a ride to the hotel," he clarified. "I'm told we're staying at the same place. May I please have a lift?"

"Saying please is always a good move," she told him.

He smiled, showing deep dimples. "I'll have to remember that for future reference."

Suspicion kept her from moving closer to him when he turned that smile on her. "How'd you know which car was mine?"

"Arizona plates." He gestured around the lot. "Everyone else here seems to be from Nevada."

"Duh. Of course Marc mentioned I'm from Arizona."

He was still smiling. "I know a lot about you, Phillipa."

That piqued her curiosity, but she refrained from indulging it. Or him. "Just get your arrogant ass into the car, Bridger."

"It's getting easier for them to breed with us, that's what I hear," Andrew said.

"That's disgusting! Where'd you hear that?" Britney asked.

"We have scientists, too," Andrew answered. "They experiment on captured ones before we kill them. The scientists are developing biological weapons to use against them."

"That's fair. They've been using science against us."

"Everything's fair in war," Andrew declared.

Michele Darabont did not know if there was any truth to Andrew's claim about Purists experimenting on vampires, and she didn't really care. She was finding this stakeout long, tiring, and boring. The fact that Andrew and Britney couldn't seem to talk about anything but vampires was the most irritating part. Their back-seat chatter almost made her wonder why she was sitting in a van outside a Las Vegas condo building. She could have been home in San Diego — but she had a mission.

"We have to kill the Abomination," she said. The compulsion to wreak havoc on vampires was more overwhelming than ever. She gripped the steering wheel tightly, almost shaking with tension. "We need to wipe the half-breeds off the face of the earth."

"Amen," Andrew said.

"There's someone coming out," Britney said. She was the one manning the high-powered binoculars. "I think it's her!"

"Let me see." Michele took the glasses from the other woman. "Where?"

"She's in the parking lot now."

It took Michele a moment to spot their quarry. Under the powerful lights of the lot, she saw a slender woman with short blond hair. "Looks like the woman from the photos."

"Kind of perky looking, for a vampire's whore," Andrew observed.

After another moment, Michele said, "No. That's not her. I think it's the whore's sister." She handed the binoculars back to Britney and sighed as the excitement of the moment drained from her. "I doubt that one has any clue to what's going on."

"Is she in their thrall too?" Andrew asked.

"Yes — she's hypnotized to see what they tell her to," Michele said.

"The poor woman," Britney said. "Wait. She's talking to someone by her car."

"One of *them?*" Andrew reached for a weapon.

"Who can tell these days?" Michele took the binoculars back and studied the man by the car. Tall, broad-shouldered, handsome, but not with the demonic beauty Michele associated with *them.* "Maybe yes, maybe not. It's hard to get an immediate reading since they started taking the daylight drugs."

"We could rescue her," Andrew declared eagerly. "She might need our help to escape the monster."

"She just invited him into her car," Michele said. "And now they're driving away." She put down the binoculars and rubbed her tired eyes.

"Should we follow them?" Andrew asked.

Michele started the van's engine. "No," she said. She yawned. "Let's call it a night. We'll get back to vampire hunting tomorrow."

CHAPTER FIVE

He was in big trouble. Matt knew it, but he was helpless to stop himself. Having Phillipa so close to him was — torture.

Magic.

The gaudy lights of the city were distracting. So were the muted thoughts and emotions of the crowds that came to him from the hotels and casinos they drove past. He closed his eyes and focused on *her.*

Even without him touching her, the warmth of her skin heated his. The slow burn of arousal glowed near the surface of her emotions. Overlaying it was a complicated mix of feelings. Some made him dizzy with desire. Others worried him. He scrupulously kept from crossing her natural mental barriers to find out what exactly was going on with her. He didn't have the right — but that didn't stop him from wanting to.

To distract them both, he chuckled.

She took the bait. "What?"

He let himself look at her. Perky, he thought, with her short blond hair, large eyes, stubborn chin, and short nose. *Why am I so attracted to someone who looks so — cute?*

"What's so funny, Bridger?"

There was a tough-as-nails quality in her voice that belied the fresh-faced American Girl looks.

"You called me arrogant," he answered. "You don't know the half of it."

She snorted.

"That's not a very ladylike sound."

"I'm no lady. And I'm not impressed by arrogance."

"But there are few as arrogant as I."

She made that sound again. "My dad and brothers are all hotshot pilots, so I had a head start even before I became a cop. The male of the species —"

"Which species is that?" he interrupted.

This amused her, but there was a dose of suspicion underlying it, which he thought healthy. She was a smart mortal, something else he found attractive.

"You know, *Homo sapiens?*"

"*Homo sapiens sapiens,*" he corrected.

"Which branch of the family tree are you from? *Homo habilis? Homo erectus?*"

"Did you just say something about an

58

erection?" he teased.

"Oh, stop it."

"You should have seen that coming."

She laughed. "You're absolutely right."

She'd been relaxing, but there was a wariness in her, and a weariness. He wondered if it was related to him at all.

"Here we are," she said, and turned into the hotel's wide driveway.

If he had any sense, he would bid her good night and leave her in the lobby. If he had any sense, he wouldn't have taken Marc's hint about hitching a ride with her. He'd known three years ago that this woman was dangerous. Correction: he'd known three years ago that he was dangerous to *her*.

"Marc told me you were shot in the line of duty recently," he said. "Are you all right?"

She brought the car to a halt underneath the ornate entrance portico and gave him a hard look as her suspicion level soared. "What else did Marc tell you?"

He gathered she wasn't happy with her brother-in-law's intrusion. He certainly didn't blame her for that. "Nothing," he replied. He put a hand out to touch her, and she shied away. "Should he have?"

"I'm fine." *God, I am so sick of telling people I'm that!*

The thought was so strong, he couldn't help but catch it. "I know what you mean," he answered.

"What?" She sounded taken aback, and angry.

"I've been injured badly enough to be fussed over by loving friends and relatives until I was ready to kill them. That's how you're feeling, isn't it?"

"I'm dealing with it," she said, the anger going out of her. "I'm better now."

She wasn't being completely truthful with him, but Bridger let it go. He opened the car door. "Thanks for the lift."

He got out, then turned to look at her. The urge to kiss her burned in him; the longing for her grew stronger than ever before. Need stretched between them.

Then the driver behind her honked impatiently, and Phillipa drove off toward the parking ramp. After her car disappeared around a curve, Matt finally entered the hotel.

The ceiling over the lobby was painted to look like blue sky dotted with fluffy clouds, with the lighting simulating soft daylight. It was never night indoors in Las Vegas. The carpet underfoot was thick and plush, in an eighteenth-century blue-and-gold pattern. Huge arrangements of fresh flowers on polished marble stands dotted the place. Though there were a lot of people around, the gigantic space didn't feel in the least bit crowded. As Matt approached the front desk, the bright, tinkling sounds of the casino came from his left; a band playing jazz reached him from a bar on the right.

As he checked in, he noticed something else — a presence so familiar that, at first, the mental energy hadn't registered as anything but more background noise. He pocketed the keycard for his room and headed toward the bar.

Mike Bleythin stared at the tumbler of amber liquid on the table as though it were a living thing that could reach out and strike him at any moment.

The small table's black surface was so polished, he could have seen his reflection in it. But since he wouldn't like what he saw — a man with dead eyes and hard features — he didn't bother looking. Instead, he concentrated on the whisky with all his finely tuned senses. All but taste. For now.

The color was sparkling shades of gold, like concentrated captured sunlight, a promise of fire in the throat. The scent was of wood and smoke. The glass was thick and heavy, the crystal rim singing a sharp note almost below even his hearing when he ran a finger around the rim.

Mike Bleythin had come to Las Vegas to kill someone. He just didn't know who, yet.

"What are you doing here, Tracker?"

He'd known there was a vampire in the bar; for some reason the town was full of them at the moment. If he'd been paying attention, he would have recognized the scent of his old friend and sometime partner right away.

"Acting like a fool," he answered as Matt Bridger sat across from him.

"Me too," Bridger said, and picked up the glass.

"Hey!" Mike complained. But the vampire gulped down the whisky anyway. "That's mine."

Bridger gave his characteristic shrug. "You weren't going to drink it."

"That's not the point."

"No use wasting twelve-year-old single malt just so you can prove that point."

"If I'm going to have an unrequited romance, it's going to be with the good stuff."

"I relate to that more than you can know."

As far as Mike knew, Bridger didn't have any addictions. Bridger glanced at a waitress, and within a minute a fresh glass of scotch was placed in front of Mike. Mike envied vampires some of their abilities. Not that his kind weren't psychically gifted, they just couldn't use telepathy with the casual ease of Bridger's kind.

"Continue torturing yourself, by all means," Bridger invited.

"It's a test of character."

"Call it what you like, it's a waste —"

"Of good whisky. I know."

"It's your life."

Bridger's edgy mood finally registered on Mike. "What's wrong, Matt?"

Bridger glanced toward the entrance and the hotel lobby beyond. Mike got the impression there was somewhere else he *needed* to be, but he was fighting the urge tooth and claw. Mike understood compulsion very well. He also knew what it usually meant for vampires.

"Who's wrong?" he amended his question.

"My dear friend and cousin," Bridger took a sip of the whisky.

"Why drink when liquor doesn't affect you?"

"I like the flavor."

"I prefer the oblivion. What about your cousin?"

Bridger took another sip. "He found his bondmate. Now he thinks everyone —

specifically me — should do the same."

"Your cousin's trying to hook you up with someone."

"His bonded's sister."

"Who is . . . not your type?" Mike guessed.

"Who is absolutely perfect. She is —" Bridger shook his head. "Everything I've been hoping I'd never find."

Mike thought he understood. "It's hard work, staying a lone wolf."

"It wasn't, until she came along."

"Maybe you shouldn't fight the urge. Aren't you a little long in the fang for one of your kind, to be without a mate?"

Bridger glanced around the bar — not that there was anyone close enough to hear their conversation, considering how low they could speak and still hear each other. "I'll thank you not to make any public references to my most attractive appendages, Bleythin."

"I won't show you mine, if you won't show me yours," Mike said. "And who am I to give advice about relationships?" Especially to another species.

"Just so," Bridger agreed. "What are you doing in town, Tracker?" he asked suspiciously. "Not looking for me, I hope? Because I'm here on Family business, and —"

"Is that why there's so many of you in

town?" Mike tapped the side of his nose. "I've been feeling like I've got a psychic sinus attack ever since I arrived."

"My happy and interfering cousin had a kid. The Family has gathered to pledge protection. It's a lot of old-fashioned, sentimental tripe, if you ask me."

"You're going to be his godfather, huh?"

"Guardian is the proper term." Bridger lifted his head proudly. "And yes, I am."

"Mazel tov." Mike picked up the drink, caught himself, and handed it to Bridger. "Have one on me."

Bridger finished off the glass, thrust it in front of Mike's face before putting it down, then asked, "What's got you playing the old 'will I or won't I get drunk' game, friend?"

"The usual," Mike answered gruffly. "Nothing you can help with."

Bridger sat back in his chair. He looked weary. Mike knew the feeling. They'd both been on the job too long.

"I wasn't going to offer," he said. He gave a quick look around. "Unless —"

"The situation doesn't involve your people."

Sometimes when vampires went bad, they took werewolves with them. When they worked together, Matt Bridger took care of the fang boys, Mike took care of the shape-shifters.

Vampires didn't always kill their renegades; they had a formal justice system and a secret prison somewhere. Werefolk weren't that complicated or civilized. Mike's job was to track down the bad ones and terminate them with extreme prejudice. He loved the hunting, and the need to kill was part of his nature. But killing his own kind wasn't. Besides, what if someday he was wrong, and he took out an innocent? Being a werewolf cop was enough to drive a man to drink.

"LVPD has been tracking a serial killer for nearly a year," he explained. "I was called in when one of our friends got a look at the case file. I haven't had a chance to look over the evidence myself yet, but from what I've heard, this has all the earmarks of classic lycanthropy. Hopefully it's a bit and not a born, 'cause with the bit I'm doing them a favor."

"Except then you'll have two to track down."

"Yeah. The bit and the one who bit him." You had to be born a vampire, but with werefolk it could go either way. "I'll worry about the details later," he told Bridger.

"You do that," Matt said, but Mike saw that he'd lost the vampire's attention.

Matt stood and walked away without a word.

True love calling? Mike wondered as he watched his friend leave the bar. "Or at least true lust."

CHAPTER SIX

"Hi, Marc. Sorry to disturb you. It's Phillipa."

"I know who it is. How are you and Matt getting along? Ow! Talk to your sister — who just swatted me on the back of the head."

"He's matchmaking, isn't he?" Phillipa asked as soon as Jo took the phone.

"Yes. We were just discussing that when you called. How are you?" Jo's voice took on sudden urgency. "He hasn't done anything — odd — has he?"

"You don't mind when I'm — odd," came Marc's deep voice from the background.

"She's my sister, and she's —"

"Excuse me," Phillipa interrupted.

"— not well," Jo finished.

"Talk to *me*," Phillipa said. "When you said that Bridger's dangerous, what did you really mean?"

Jo's words had been nagging at Phillipa

68

since she'd left the party — her cop's sixth sense at work. She had the impression that there was some secret meaning her sister was forbidden to impart yet wanted to share. She wondered what Jo would have to say if Marc wasn't there.

She knew she was being paranoid, but it also frightened her to think that her cop sense might be as screwed up as the rest of her. She'd grown so anxious about what she sensed that she hadn't even waited to reach her room before calling Jo. She was leaning against a white marble pillar near the elevators, holding her cell phone to her ear.

"Dangerous as in —" Jo began.

"Tell her he was in the military," Marc's voice cut across Jo's. "In the SAS. He's very patriotic. And he loves his mother."

Phillipa sighed. This was not going anywhere. "I'll talk to you tomorrow," she said, and ended the call. She started to turn off the phone, but it rang before she could. "Hello? Hi, Pete. How are you? How's your investigation coming along?"

A wave of relief went through her as she listened to the answers from Peter Martin, her friend on the local police force. Pete was nice. Pete was normal. They had a lot in common. Common ground and normalcy were far more important than the exotic allure of the mysterious Matthias Bridger.

"Did I hear my name taken in vain?"

"Gotta go," Phillipa said, and switched the phone off as she stepped away from the column to face Bridger. "Are you in the SAS?"

"Who dares, wins," he answered. "That's our motto."

"Cool." She sounded like a star-struck kid, but she couldn't help it. She couldn't help it if she had a thing for the military; the tougher the service, the better. It was hard to get tougher than Britain's Special Air Service. "Unofficial motto, Train hard, fight easy."

"And Speed, Aggression, Surprise," he added, with a knowing grin. "Do you want to see my tattoo?"

"I'll show you mine if you show me yours," she blurted out.

And realized that one of his hands was possessively cradling the back of her head, and that she was leaning back, enjoying his touch. His other hand clasped hers. His thumb was slowly stroking across the back of her wrist, sending sparks and shivers all through her.

Oh, God, here they went again! She should stop this right now! Then she looked into his eyes, and all there was in the world was heat.

The next thing she knew, they were in the elevator, their hands on each other. "Isn't this where we started?" she asked.

"Can't be helped," he answered. "You belong to me."

If she'd been the least bit rational, this statement would have made her furious. Instead, a thrill swept through her.

When the elevator stopped, she barely noticed that it wasn't on her floor. She stopped thinking altogether when he picked her up and carried her down the hallway. She closed her eyes, breathed in the scent of him, and just let it happen.

Goddess, she smelled so good!

The weight of her was perfect in his arms, though she was more slender than he remembered. Three years of fighting the hunger had been too long; he couldn't wait another moment. Her arms were around his neck, and he turned his head and bit into the soft flesh of her wrist. Even though they were in a public hotel hallway, he couldn't stop himself from tasting her.

Sweet. Though not so sweet as he remembered. *Still just as hot.*

Her sigh of pleasure brushed across his cheek, warm and enticing. The orgasm that rushed through her echoed through him. It gave him pleasure to give her pleasure, and increased his need. The rich taste of her blood tantalized, but only having her body, essence, and spirit could completely satisfy his primal need.

Primal, he heard her think. *Prime. Where have I heard that before?*

He was barely able to stop the impulse to kick open the door when they reached his room. He put Phillipa down but held her close while he unlocked the door.

"I have a confession to make," he said when they were inside his bedroom.

"You don't have an SAS winged dagger tattoo," she responded.

"It actually represents Excalibur." He kissed her throat, then her chin. "You remember me naked from last time?" he whispered in her ear.

She ran her hands up his back and shoulders, and his jacket slipped to the floor. Then she began working on his shirt button. The woman had a talent for undressing him.

"No," she said. "But you wouldn't have acknowledged being SAS if you weren't out of the game."

"That game," he admitted.

"Wearing ink would call attention. The

SAS never calls attention to itself, unless you're shooting at someone."

"Even then, the encounters are generally brief and not remembered by the ones encountered. You're a military groupie, aren't you?" he asked.

"I am *in* the military," she answered. "Was."

Her bitterness wasn't lost on him. "I might consider this conversation strange, if I were talking to anyone else I wanted to have enormous amounts of sex with."

"How so?" she asked. "And how enormous?"

He chuckled wickedly. "That remains to be seen."

She put her hand over his when he reached for the light switch. "I don't need to see anything." She slid her hand up his bare back and through his hair. "I only need to feel."

She pulled his head down, and her mouth found his before he could question her. He let the awareness of her apprehension go in the wash of sensation from her kiss. What did it matter if she was being shy? He could see in the dark, anyway.

What about your *tattoo?* He thought. *Here.*

She placed his palm on the center of her

flat stomach. He felt the heat of bruises surrounding the mark, and knew why she didn't want him to see. Recovery was so much easier for his kind when they were injured that it was easy to forget that damage could be mental as well as physical to their more fragile mortal cousins. And healing both could take longer.

"You are the most beautiful thing in my world," he told her, and carried her to the bed.

How sweet, Phillipa thought, and held on tight. As they stretched out together, she savored the solid reality of him, his strength, his warmth.

You're really here.

I'm really here.

It seemed as natural as breathing to share her thoughts with him.

"I've waited too long for this," he said as his hands caressed her.

For a moment she was angry for the time lost between them, but arousal overcame it. And it was lust rather than temper that caused her to sink her nails into the taut muscles of his back.

Matt gasped, then laughed, overjoyed at the fierceness of her lovemaking. A sharp, quick nip on her breast brought him the taste of her. She returned the favor by biting his shoulder.

Do that again, he told her. *Make me bleed.*

She responded with a harder bite, drawing a little blood. Her tongue lapped across his skin like a cat just discovering cream.

He had the advantage of fangs, and he used them. He'd never been so hungry, or so satisfied. Yet not sated. He could go on tasting her forever, and not just her blood.

Matt took his time kissing and touching his way all over her body, and kept his growing desire under tight control.

Come for me again, he thought every time a fresh orgasm took her, caressing her until he made it happen. Her skin grew slick with sweat, and he loved the salty sweet taste. She moaned and shook, and ground her body against his. He was hard and hot and needy, but he didn't stop arousing her.

Not yet.

Though he shook with the effort, he waited until she shouted, "Enough!"

"Should I stop?"

"Don't you dare."

"Enough what? Be specific. Can you say please?"

"No. Make love to me, already!"

His answering shout was half laughter and

half triumph. Sliding inside her was the greatest satisfaction he'd ever known. Possessing her drove him into frenzy. The world became an inferno as he pounded into her.

When release finally came, it was with a mutual explosion that was more than ecstasy. Matt felt like he was dying, and taking her down into the dark with him — only to be reborn. And she was still with him.

After all that, all he could do was hold her tight and go to sleep.

When he awoke many hours later, Phillipa was gone.

Fair's fair, he though, since he'd walked out on her the first time.

But he was still furious with her for leaving.

CHAPTER SEVEN

"What the hell was I thinking?" Phillipa moaned.

"You went to bed with him again, didn't you?" Jo accused her.

"Oh, yeah." Her body was still buzzing from the pleasure.

"What were you thinking?"

"I *wasn't* thinking. What's the matter with me?"

"Where should I start?" Jo answered.

Phillipa pulled her cell phone away from her ear and glared into it, as if her sister could see her. Then she shifted on the edge of her bed, sighed, and held the phone back to her ear. Much of the contents of her large purse and a small suitcase were scattered around her on the bed. She was so rattled that she wasn't sure if she was preparing to flee the scene or get ready for this afternoon's ceremony. She was scattered, confused. Dazed.

And thoroughly pissed at herself for once again succumbing to her totally devastating attraction to Matt Bridger.

"I'm sorry I called," she told her sister. "You've got enough on your mind without having me whine at you."

Phillipa prided herself on not being a whiner. She was self-sufficient, sure of herself, in control. Or she had been.

"I've got to get *me* back," she said. "Being around Bridger is not helping."

"Very good point," Jo said. "He's rather well known in his family for not being the settling-down kind."

"Who wants to settle down?" Phillipa protested. "I just want — to stop wanting him, I guess."

"Oh, crap. You've been carrying a torch for three years, haven't you?"

"I wouldn't put it like that."

Even if it was the truth.

"It's not like I've been thinking about the guy," Phillipa explained. "It's more of a visceral thing. It's like a physical craving that has nothing to do with my brain. My body —" She sighed again. "My body doesn't need the distraction right now."

Since she was on eight different medications, and had a calendar full of medical appointments. But right now, her sister had a

78

newborn baby, and a passel of in-laws visiting her.

"I shouldn't have called. I'm sorry. What can I do to help today? Do Mom and Dad need picking up at the airport?"

"They do. You can. But let's get back to why you called."

"That's okay. I don't —"

"So, you slept with Bridger again. How come you're not still with him? Did he walk out on you?"

"I walked out. Ran, really," Phillipa admitted. "I woke up realizing that I can't deal with any more complications, and I pretty much panicked. I reacted like a total wuss."

And now I have to face this guy in a few hours, at my nephew's christening. And he and I are going to be the godparents.

"Oh, crap," she muttered. "This is going to be awkward."

"You mean the ceremony? Nonsense," Jo stated firmly. "You'll both perform your part without any fuss or bother. Won't you?"

Phillipa caught the adamant tone of her sister's voice. "Yes, ma'am," she acknowledged. "You sound just like Mom."

"Thank you."

"Maybe I could get Pete to come as my date." Phillipa shook her head, instantly ashamed of herself. "No, that wouldn't be fair to him. It's not right to use a friend."

"It might not be safe, either. You *do not* want to make a man like Bridger jealous."

Phillipa gave a shaky laugh. "I doubt he'd be jealous. We've got a physical attraction, but nothing more. Besides, there's Octavia. I'm sure she'll be vying for his attention."

And what was that emotion curdling in her stomach? Certainly not jealousy, she hoped. *No complications. No entanglements. Be grateful if Octavia wants him.*

"Grrr . . ."

"What's that?"

"Nothing," Phillipa answered. "I'm just crazy."

"Well, stop it. Take a cold shower."

"Good idea."

"Then go to the airport," Jo ordered. "And don't you dare be late getting to the ceremony."

"Let me help you."

Phillipa kept walking across the hot tarmac. She'd spotted the man coming up behind her when she'd pulled into the parking lot. His car had been following hers, but she wasn't sure for how long. Her cop senses were definitely not working at the moment.

He moved closer. "You're in danger."

80

She pretended not to hear. The Las Vegas airport was one of the busiest in the world, and this end, the area her sister called the Whaleport, was especially noisy with the steady traffic of small corporate and private planes. There were a lot of cars and hotel limos waiting in front of the building, but she didn't see anyone but herself and the nut behind her walking across the lot. Not that she was particularly worried.

"They haven't corrupted you yet," the nutjob went on. "But it's only a matter of time. It's dangerous for me to be talking to you. I'm under orders not to approach, but it's wrong not to try to save the innocent. Your sister's already damned, and —"

"All right. That's it." Phillipa spun around to face the nut.

He stopped suddenly, stumbling when he almost ran into her. He was young and clean, and dressed respectably. His eyes were wide with surprise and his expression was intense, but Phillipa didn't detect any immediate signs that he was on drugs.

"What is the matter with you?" she demanded. "What about my sister?"

"It's not really her fault, but she's beyond saving now. He made her what she is," he answered.

"Who?"

"The vampire."

Good lord. He was a rambling maniac who'd been out in the Nevada sun too long.

He came closer, his voice dropping to a whisper. "The vampires are after you, too," he confided. "They want all our beautiful women to be their sex slaves."

"Do they?" she answered, backing a step. She clutched her car keys between her fingers in case she needed a defensive weapon. "Well, that's mighty selfish of them."

He nodded, the sarcasm lost on him. "It's not too late for you. You can help us destroy the vampires. You can get revenge for what they've done to your sister. And —"

He suddenly looked like a deer caught in headlights, and backed hastily away.

"Hi, hon. Who's your friend?"

Phillipa turned at the sound of her father's voice. For once she was glad that her father was always too impatient to wait to be met at the baggage claim area. Her parents had come looking for her, towing their wheeled luggage behind them.

"That was no friend." When she glanced back, the stranger's van was backing out of its parking space. She was annoyed that she couldn't make out the license plate number with her current vision problems.

"He looked like a loon," her mother observed.

Mom was a veteran detective. "Nothing gets past you," Phillipa told her. She accepted a kiss on the cheek from her father, and took her mother's bag. "We better get going. Jo will have my head if we're not at the ceremony on time."

"May I have a moment of your time, Marcus?"

"Your tone is civilized, Matthias," Marc Cage answered him. "But that's not what your eyes say."

"I am Prime. We aren't civilized."

He followed Marc into a small office off the hall entrance where the guests were gathering.

When they had a bit more privacy, Marc asked. "You hung over?"

Matt didn't completely know what a hangover felt like to a mortal, but he supposed he was experiencing the vampire equivalent. If it was possible to have too much sex, he'd had it. He'd taken blood, and given it, and done too much of that, as well.

"Damn," he muttered. "The woman is —"

He shook his head. Some things were meant to be kept private. Even though he'd shared memories of sexual exploits with his cousin before, this was different. Phillipa was different.

"Damn," he said again.

Marcus nodded. "That's the Elliot women, all right."

"You are not taking this seriously."

"I'm dead serious. You do anything to hurt my bondmate's sister, and you'll answer to me for it."

Knowing the first reaction for a Prime was to snarl at the threat, Marcus stepped back, let him show a bit of fang and claw, and waited for him to calm down.

Within moments Bridger took a deep breath and gave an acknowledging nod. "Fair is fair to take care of your family. Besides, I couldn't bear to see her hurt." He pointed sternly at Marc. "And *that*, cousin, is the point."

Marcus looked disgusted. "Not that old song again. When you find your bondmate, you have to live with the gift the goddess grants you. Even if it is inconvenient."

"It isn't inconvenient for me. It's dangerous."

Marc smiled. "But you're not denying she is your bondmate. That's a good start."

"There is no *start*. I cannot allow it to happen, for her sake. For her protection."

"Bullshit. That excuse has always been bullshit. It was convenient when you were younger, but you're past a hundred now — your mind, your body, and your soul need completion. You'll never be happy until —"

"I don't care about being happy," Matt cut him off. "I don't need to be happy. Not for what it could cost the woman I bond with."

Marc sneered. "Could. Would. Should. If. What the hell do any of them have to do with what *is?* Cope with what happens, not with what might happen."

"Easy for you to say, when you haven't made the kind of enemies I have."

"Do you want to break her heart?"

Marc's words hurt him, but Matt answered. "Better that than to hold her broken body in my arms." It was an old argument, and not worth continuing. "I know you mean well, but you've put me, and the girl, in a very dangerous position. I won't see her again after today, but there might still be repercussions. If there's any trouble, it's because you brought it on her. It will be up to you to protect her."

"Protect her yourself. She's your bond-mate."

Matt shook his head and backed away. "Let it go, Marcus. Leave me alone."

"She needs you as much as you need her."

"Leave her alone, too."

He wasn't aware of the couple standing by the doorway until he turned. The fact that he hadn't detected their presence was a stark sign of how badly Phillipa was affecting his senses. He had known the instant she arrived at the hall door, and nothing else but the struggle not to go to her had mattered to him.

"Octavia," he acknowledged with a nod. It wasn't easy to even pretend politeness to the Prime with her. "Sandor's son."

"Jason," Octavia said, eyes flashing angrily. "His name is Jason Cage. To call him by his sire's name is the rudest thing I've ever heard." The shudder she gave was more mental than physical. "It reminds me of my own origins."

Octavia had been born into one of the old repressive, patriarchal vampire tribes. Fortunately for her, the tribe had been absorbed into the matriarchal Family Caeg when she was still young.

The Prime put his hand on Octavia's shoulder, though his bright blue gaze never left Matt's. "Perhaps you don't know that Matthias is the one who apprehended me. He'll never see me as anything but houseless and nameless. Will you, Matt?"

"You did your time," Matt answered. Because Marc was looking at him sternly, Matt managed as polite a nod as he could. "We are both guests here. The mistake was mine."

He wondered how much Octavia and this *other* Cage cousin had overheard. Did he need to count Jason Cage as one of his enemies? Was Jason interested in revenge for a punishment he'd claimed was unjust?

Matt stepped forward to warn Jason off his woman, but Marc was there before him. He put his arm around the other Prime and asked, "What were you in for anyway, Jase?"

"Practicing sorcery without a license," was the prompt answer.

"Considering what you do for a living now, I don't see the problem."

"Times were different then," Jason answered.

"And magic was less profitable," Octavia put in.

Jason's infraction had been far more than just using magic, but Matt forced himself to laugh with everyone else to help break the tension.

"Your bondmate asked us to tell you that everyone is now here," Octavia said. "It's time for the ceremony to begin."

Chapter Eight

"This doesn't make a lot of sense to me, Jo."

Jo sighed with frustration. "Mom."

"For one thing, why aren't we using the actual church instead of the church's meeting hall? The sacristy has a perfectly good baptismal font, doesn't it?"

"I'm sure it does," Jo answered. "But, you see —"

"And why is Marc's grandmother officiating?"

"Because she's the matri — matriarch of the family."

"I don't understand."

"We don't have to understand, we just have to appreciate being asked to take part," Dad chimed in. "Do you have something against diversity all of a sudden, darling?"

"Of course not," Mom defended herself. "I'm curious. I'm a detective. I'm supposed to be curious."

"Our part is to sit down and be quiet," Dad went on. "Stop badgering your daughter, Connie."

"When have I ever badgered anyone, Matthew?"

Keeping her attention on her family kept Phillipa from marching up to Matthias Bridger and telling him he was hers and nobody else's.

The longing to be with Matt was so strong it was an actual physical ache. It was as though the need had gotten into her blood and bones and being. And since she already had a nasty disease mucking up her body, she didn't need this other crap that had to do with wanting sex with Matt Bridger. The weirdest thing was, even though she couldn't see him, she was certain of his exact whereabouts.

"I'm crazy," she muttered, her hands clenching at her sides.

When he came into the hall, she *knew,* even before she looked up.

"You're not crazy," Jo leaned close and whispered in her ear.

Yes, you are, another voice said in her head. *We both are.*

She glowered at Bridger. The last thing she needed was *him* telling her she was crazy. Then, the fact that she was outraged tickled her sense of humor. Imagining voices in her head was a certain amount of proof that she *was* crazy. Or at least that she hadn't gotten enough sleep lately.

"We can start now," Jo said. "Mom, Dad, come with me."

The three of them moved up the aisle and took seats in the front left row. Everybody else not participating in the ceremony was already seated. This left Phillipa standing alone in the back of the hall, paralyzed with the sinking realization that she was supposed to be standing next to the man she was trying so hard not to go near.

She managed to plaster a smile on her face and make her feet move forward. This was for her sister, and her nephew, and there was no way she would fail in her duty to her family. Or embarrass them in front of the whole Cage crew. She became acutely aware that everyone was looking at her.

And that many of them were *thinking* at her, which made no sense, but which seemed to be standard operating procedure with Marcus's family.

Then her gaze locked onto Bridger's, and the expression in those cool green eyes steadied her, and gave her a boost of confidence she hadn't realized she needed.

She couldn't remember having rehearsed this, but somehow she knew what to do.

At the front of the hall was a table covered in rich black velvet. Velvet as the night, she thought. Faceted crystals were scattered across it, representing stars. There was a golden statue of a woman with uplifted arms, holding an orb of milky translucent moonstone to one side. Next to the moon goddess was a smaller statue of a delicately wrought golden tree, its branches bare, a small door incised at the base of the trunk. In the center of the table sat a shallow golden basin containing water. On one side of it was a small, ornately carved cinnabar box full of dust. On the other side was a jewel-encrusted silver goblet. For a moment, Phillipa thought she caught the scent of blood and spice. Then she realized that whatever was in the goblet must be a heavily fragrant wine. Thick white candles in shiny onyx holders burned on both ends of the table. Phillipa wasn't sure about the symbolism, but she recognized an altar when she faced one.

The baby's paternal great-grandmother stood on the opposite side of the altar. She wore a midnight blue shawl richly embroidered with a gold tree and silver moon pattern, and held the baby in her arms. Brandon was wrapped in a bright red satin cloth, also richly embroidered.

Phillipa agreed with her mother that this was the strangest baptism she'd ever seen, but the disturbing thought was instantly soothed away. Though the trappings were strange, this was sacred, and the responsibility she was accepting was a grave one.

This knowledge came to her while the Matri looked into her eyes, deep into her soul. Phillipa could only answer with a solemn nod of understanding and assent.

"The mother of us all blesses you," the old woman said, and her attention turned to Bridger.

Phillipa wasn't sure how long she'd been standing beside him, or when they'd clasped hands. But she became acutely aware of his presence as the Matri studied him.

It wasn't his strong, squarely built body in the perfectly tailored dark suit, or his rugged handsomeness, or the way he exuded danger with a sexual charge to it, that she noticed now. There was a seriousness about him, and a tender, protective look in his eyes when his gaze shifted to the baby. The brief glimpse of gentleness nearly melted Phillipa.

Her attention was called back to the

ceremony when the baby was handed across the altar to her. She carefully unwrapped Brandon from the satin blanket and turned with the naked infant to face Bridger. Matt put one hand on the baby's chest, and supported his back with the other.

While they held him, the old woman sprinkled Brandon's bare skin with a bit of dirt, then a few drops of water. The baby squirmed and cried for a moment, then settled down.

Then Matt dipped a finger in the goblet and held it to Brandon's mouth. The baby suckled the liquid off his finger and smiled up at Bridger. The Matri chuckled, and there was scattered applause from some of the guests.

"This child is of our Family," the Matri declared. "How do we protect one of our own?"

"All through the night," Matt responded.

"All through the day," Phillipa said.

"I will teach him the secrets of the night," Matt said.

"He will learn how to dwell in the day," Phillipa said.

"You swear to be his guardians?" the Matri asked.

"I swear by the mistress of the moon," Matt answered.

"I swear by the lord of light," Phillipa promised.

"In the midnight hour and the noonday heat?"

"At all times and places," they replied together.

"You will protect him from the hands of his enemies?"

"His enemies are mine."

"Even when his enemy is himself?"

"To teach him, to guide him, to admonish him, to love and nurture him, is my duty."

"So you swear, Matthias, son of House Lorelei of the Family Caeg-Bruca?"

"I swear."

"So you swear, Phillipa, daughter of House Constance and Matthew of Family Elliot?"

"I swear."

The Matri looked from them to the people gathered behind them. "It is sworn. Do you witness?"

"So we witness," a chorus of voices solemnly replied.

She took the baby from them and held him up for all to see. "So is guardianship sworn for Brandon Cage-Elliot, of House Josephine and Marcus, of Family Caeg. I proclaim it!"

Then everyone was on their feet, applauding and congratulating Jo and Marc, who came and took the baby from his great-grandmother.

CHAPTER NINE

Surrounded by people, Phillipa felt all the energy drain from her, and suddenly absolutely nothing about the ceremony made any sense. A shiver of fear went through her, and her head began to spin.

Strong hands came around her, and she found herself leaning back into a protective embrace. "Give it a moment," Bridger soothed. "Just close your eyes."

She did, which made her more aware of him. And that was fine. After the moment passed, she didn't care that everything else was weird. She felt fine.

"Nice," she said, and sighed as every bit of tension melted away.

"You're heavy," he answered.

"You're a wimp."

There was something so nice about the way they fit together. "Do you want me to stand on my own?"

"No."

"Then stop complaining."

"I could bicker with you for hours."

Oddly enough, this reminded her of the comfortably quarrelsome way her parents occasionally talked to each other, and that was just . . . wrong. It wasn't like she and Bridger had that kind of long-term relationship, or any sort of relationship at all.

When she tried to move away, he continued to hold her close.

Matt was totally enamored of the scent of Phillipa's skin, the touch of her hair against his cheek, and the way she fitted into his embrace. Dangerous, he knew. Stupid. But for this one last time, the closeness felt so good. When she tried to move away from him, he almost compulsively held her tighter.

He recognized that his possessiveness made her nervous — but only because she liked it, when a modern, independent woman wasn't supposed to like that sort of thing.

Her attitude both amused and bemused him, but when all her muscles tensed, he made himself let her go. What either of them liked or wanted could not matter.

"You know I'm doing this for your own good, right?" he asked.

Phillipa whirled to face him. "What?"

He made a dismissive gesture. "Never mind. Talking to myself, really, love."

"Don't you 'love' me!"

She seemed as surprised by her vehemence as he was. Whatever was going on between them was even harder and more confusing for her than it was for him.

Instead of trying to explain, he replied, "I'm working on that."

"Good." She turned to walk away, and suddenly there was Sandor-Jason Cage standing in front of her. Smiling. With a Prime's avid glint in his eyes.

"We haven't had a chance to meet before now, and I'm very sorry for the lost time," he said, smoothly taking Phillipa's hand. "I had to work last night, so I couldn't make it to the party. I'm one of the few Cages that actually live in town. Perhaps —"

"She doesn't want to spend time with you," Matt declared, stepping up to stand beside Phillipa.

Phillipa gave him an annoyed glance.

Jason acted like he wasn't there. "You performed the ceremony very well," he flattered her. "Especially since you must find our traditions old-fashioned."

"Some of us respect our traditions," Matt reminded the other Prime.

98

"Some of us are complete fools, too," Jason answered.

Whatever was going on between the two men, Phillipa was certain the antagonism had nothing to do with her. Not from the way they were suddenly glaring daggers at each other.

Tension radiated out from the pair to the rest of the room as well. Everyone stared. Bodies went still. Voices went quiet.

Phillipa jerked her hand from the man's grasp. "It's so lovely feeling like a bone between a pair of big dogs." She walked away in disgust without sparing either of the antagonists another look.

"Primes," Jo murmured, when Phillipa reached her and their mother at the back of the crowd. "Don't pay them any mind. Marc will straighten it out."

"I don't care if it gets straightened out or not," Phillipa said. "Except that bloodshed at Brandon's christening would be extremely rude."

"You'd be surprised, with this bunch," Jo said.

Phillipa risked a quick glance back at Bridger, and, yep, her heart jolted at the sight of him facing the other man, his expression cold but his eyes full of fire and fury.

What was it with her and dangerous men? She forced herself to look away.

Mom was holding Brandon easily on her hip. Phillipa kissed him on the forehead and walked toward the hall entrance. The Cages made her crazy, Matt Bridger most of all. She had to get out of this macho, charged atmosphere right now.

Only to discover Pete Martin coming in the door as she reached it.

I have too many men in my life, she thought.

But it's all about the life in your men.

Where had that thought come from? And why had the voice in her mind sounded like Octavia's?

"Hey, looks like I made it after all," Pete said with a grin.

"What are you doing here?" she asked, worried that perhaps she'd done something stupid and called him after vowing not to during the panic attack she'd had earlier in the day.

"Your sister called and invited me," he answered.

Phillipa shot a surprised look at Jo. She wasn't used to her younger sister interfering in her life, but she couldn't help sighing with relief. "How thoughtful of her," she said, turning back to Pete.

"Yeah. Am I in time?"

She put her arm through his and turned him back toward the door. "The ceremony's just over. Let's go get a cup of coffee."

"But — don't you want me to meet your family?"

She gave as airy a laugh as she could manage. "Not at the moment." She leaned close to his ear and whispered. "Madness runs in Marc's family, and right now I think it's entered a marathon."

"You know, boys," Marc said, getting between Matt and Jason, "this might not be the best time."

"Oh, Marcus, let them have their fun," the Matri said.

"Don't encourage them, Mother," Marc's mother complained.

Matt heard everyone talking, but his focus was on getting his temper under control. Having the eye contact with the other Prime broken helped. He glared at Marc's back and told himself the hostility raging through him was because he disliked Jason Cage, and not the bonding urge trying to take over his life.

"Don't be such a spoilsport," the Matri told her daughter. "Don't you remember what it feels like when a pair of Primes draw blood over your affections?"

"I don't see that it matters," Octavia spoke up. "Since the object of affection has left the building."

Matt snarled in frustration and pushed Marc out of his way, but he could feel Phillipa's absence before seeing that she was nowhere in sight.

"With another man," Octavia added. "A mortal, I believe."

He started to go after Phillipa, but Josephine stepped in front of him before he reached the door. He was so frantic, he might have pushed her aside if she hadn't been holding the baby.

"Stop right now," she said, totally undaunted by the fierce look he gave her. "Come to your senses. I will not have you screwing over my sister any more than you already have."

"I haven't done anything —"

"She told me all about last night."

"That is none of your —"

"Oh, yes it is." Josephine jabbed a finger against his chest. "Marc's told me all about your reputation with mortal women. You are not a nice man, Matthias Bridger. Tomcatting around is fine for vampires, but my sister is a mortal. She left with a nice *mortal* man. Get over her. Leave her alone." She gestured at the crowd. "Why don't you take Octavia home?"

Though something in his blood and bones fought against her words, the sane part of him knew she was right.

He nodded acquiescence to this woman who was now head of House Josephine of Family Caeg. "All right." He turned around, looking at the female vampires standing around them. "Maybe I will take Octavia home."

Jason laughed. "Not if I have anything to say about it."

"Oh, goody, bloodshed," Octavia murmured. "For *moi.*"

Goody, indeed, Matt thought with a toothy smile. Because he was *really* spoiling for a fight, now.

CHAPTER TEN

Mike Bleythin liked Las Vegas normally, but the number of vampires in the area at the moment was stuffing up his senses something awful. And taking an antihistamine wasn't going to be any help, as the sense affected most by their proximity wasn't really his sensitive nose.

Nice enough people, vampires, when they were on your side. But their concentrated presence was damned hard on other psychically sensitive species. Especially when they were being rowdy.

The mental static had gotten so intense in the middle of the afternoon that Mike had literally had to get out of town. Now here he was out in the desert, seated on a rock and watching the neon beauty of the city coming out to strut as the sun faded away. He would be relieved when the guest vamps cleared out of town, so he could filter the remaining locals out of his consciousness.

He liked Vegas. He liked vampires. He hated his job and wished he was home. That was the pack creature in him coming out. He glanced up at the darkening sky.

"If the moon was full, I'd probably want to howl at it," he muttered. Even then, a howl was best done with the rest of the pack.

But he hadn't come out into the countryside just to get away from the headache and the white noise. Or to feel sorry for himself. Mike stood, stretched, and took a long, deep breath.

He scented death in the air, but most of what he detected was simply the residue of the normal order of things. He was searching for death that didn't belong out here in the desert past the fringes of the city. Of course, he wasn't going to find what he was looking for while in this form. Even though his senses were far keener than a normal human's, mortal olfactory equipment simply wasn't designed for the fine-tuned work he needed to do.

He'd been reluctant to change while it was still light, but now that it was dark, he still hesitated. Simply because being in wolf form called to him with the same kind of dangerous power as alcohol. Mike Bleythin hated being tempted by anything. Sex, drugs, rock and roll. Chasing rabbits. Some deeply regretted youthful indiscretions had taught him that *everything* tempted him to lose control. If it wasn't for the anchor of family, friends, and the duty he'd sworn to, he'd probably take off to one of the remote reserves and join the small pack of were-wolves who lived in morphed form permanently. It was — tempting.

Mike sneered, then stripped off his clothes and concealed them at the base of the boulder. The Bleythins were a black wolf pack, and that was what he changed into; two hundred pounds of black-furred alpha menace.

It felt really good.

So good, in fact, that he allowed himself to howl — something werewolves outside the private reserves rarely did. Because, frankly, the sound was too eerie and scary for humans to mistake it for what it really was: death on four legs, controlled by the intelligence of a man. That sound used to call up mobs of armed villagers in the old days. Of course, no one believed in were-wolves anymore.

The villagers were all in the casinos, where they couldn't tell day from night. And that left the wide, moonlight-bathed desert landscape beyond the last of the sprawling suburbs free for him to roam.

At least for a little while.

All this sentimental and romantic rubbish about the good old days ran quickly through Mike's head, then sensibly settled back into the dark recesses, where it wouldn't get in the way of self-preservation. Or the fact that he was out here to do his job.

He tuned all his senses for evidence of a werewolf kill of the best and most dangerous prey of all.

Though it happened rarely these days, there were many reasons why werefolk attacked humans.

Frequently it was done in a fit of full-moon mania by someone who didn't know how to control the change. If you were born a were, this wasn't a problem. It was the few humans who survived a werefolk bite that were affected by the moon change. They had no control when they morphed, and were the ones most likely to attack others.

Changing humans used to be done under controlled conditions, for the sake of the werefolk gene pools. Now it was forbidden, even considered a perversion. But since when did forbidding a thing stop it? When a forced change happened, Mike's job was to capture the changed creature for rehabilitation, if possible, and kill the natural shape-shifter responsible for the infection.

But when they killed, moon-mad were-wolves didn't have sense enough to hide the bodies. From what he'd recently learned from his LVPD source, this killer had carefully concealed the corpses.

For awhile Mike sat quietly and simply breathed, his senses now greatly enhanced. When the wind finally brought a faint impression to him, he silently stalked off. He circled the area warily, losing and gaining the scent several times, carefully aware of every other living creature in the vicinity. Once he was certain he was the only sentient being within miles, Mike concentrated on his quarry.

What he found was in a crevice at the top of a hill. There was a hint of decay in the air, but Mike caught a lingering trace of fear as well. The victim had been brought here still alive. It wasn't hard for him to find a few pitiful bones, or to realize they'd been gnawed on. He had not just a man-killer on his paws, but a man-eater, as well.

In other words, he had an old-fashioned lycanthrope to find, before the villagers came rushing out of the casinos with torches and pitchforks and weapons of mass destruction that would be aimed at all his kind.

Shit.

The world went black for just a moment; Mike's body tensed and his head lifted sharply.

Then he smelled the cigarette.

"Must you?" a voice asked.

"I don't know why you object to my bad habits, you're not likely to die of second-hand smoke," another voice replied.

Why the hell hadn't he sensed them approaching? There was a werewolf there. And a vampire. And they were practically on top of him, casually strolling up the hill. But he couldn't move.

"He's here, isn't he?" the werewolf asked.

The vampire laughed. "You really are the world's only mind-blind wolf, aren't you?"

"Around you, who wouldn't be?"

"You flatter me," the vampire said. "However . . ."

Pain stabbed through Mike's mind. After that, everything came through a growing screen of psychic white noise. He fell to the ground, paralyzed. Soon the pair was standing over him. One of them nudged him with a foot.

"It's a good thing you talked me into coming out here tonight," the vampire said.

"Haven't you read the research on serial killers?" the werewolf asked. "The profilers say we like to revisit our kill sites. I knew he'd be out here," the werewolf added. "This is where I'd come if I were looking for me."

"It's a good thing you found out that this one's in town," the vampire said. "I was beginning to believe that Matthias really was only in Vegas for the brat's ceremony. This pair always works as a team."

"And they're after us," the werewolf said.

"You, definitely. Us, possibly," the vampire said. "But soon no one is going to be interested in our activities whatsoever."

Paralyzed, Mike felt hands on him, running through his fur like he was some kind of puppy dog that would be happy for a petting. It was obscene. Wrong. The mind behind that touch was terribly, terribly strong.

Magic. Wizardry. Sorcery. These were the old terms for what this one had.

The modern world might define it as a strong will and lack of ethics. But whatever you called it, it was very, very dangerous. And Mike was trapped in the grip of that will. As much as he tried to morph, or even move, he was held in place, held in form.

"Can I kill him?" the werewolf asked.

"Can you?" the vampire wondered. "Even as blood-hungry as you are, can you kill one of your own kind? I know I couldn't."

There was a long silence, apparently while the werewolf considered the worst thing any supernatural being could do to another.

"He could kill me," the werewolf finally said. He sounded like he was pouting.

"But he is an aberration."

"I kill people!" the werewolf protested, as though his courage had been called into question.

"There's no reason for you not to," the vampire soothed. "They're *only* people."

"Yeah," the werewolf agreed. "Who cares about mortals?"

"They are delicious, but disposable," the vampire said. "But do we have a right to destroy our own kind?" The vampire sounded downright righteous.

"You're not going to let me kill him, are you?"

"For the sake of your soul — no."

"Then what are we going to do with him?"

"For the sake of his soul, I'm going to give him a gift."

The vampire that had been holding his mind all along, keeping him still, not letting him morph, had also been searching, delicately probing. Now, delicacy was replaced by white-hot pain.

Faintly, somewhere a world away, Mike

heard the werewolf ask, "What are you doing?"

"Giving him what he wants," the vampire answered.

Then the world went from white-hot to freezing black.

CHAPTER ELEVEN

"What do you mean, you talked to her?" Michele demanded when Andrew confessed to what he'd done. "Do you know how dangerous it could be to talk to one of them?"

"She isn't one of them," Andrew answered adamantly. "She's an innocent bystander. We can save her."

"He means he has a crush on her because she's an attractive blond." Britney's voice was full of scathing sarcasm.

"Where did you talk to this woman? When?" Michele asked.

"Nowhere near the vampires' territory," Andrew said. "I was careful. She's a good person, I could tell."

"Beauty doesn't equal goodness," Britney said. She sneered at Andrew. "Those creatures exist to corrupt beauty, remember?"

"Maybe we should think more about redemption than destruction."

Britney laughed. "Vampires are perversions of nature. Or has a pretty face made you forget that?"

"She isn't a vampire. She doesn't even believe in vampires."

"So she just thought you were crazy," Britney said.

"I guess. I think she could help us rescue her sister and the baby. Maybe if the child was raised —"

"That isn't a child, it's a monster. We have to protect our own kind."

Michele paced across the living room of the small apartment while the pair argued, trying to burn off frustrated energy, and vehemently wished she was somewhere else. A news program played on the television against one wall, and her gaze strayed to the screen, welcoming the distraction. This operation was dangerously close to spinning totally out of her control.

She appreciated the Purists' commitment, but their attitudes were totally amateurish. They were preparing to go up against vampires, not go door to door delivering political pamphlets!

She turned back to the others. "Andrew, the brat and its mother die. You're to stay away from the sister. Britney, stop sniping at Andrew. Focus, people!"

Britney popped up off the couch, fairly quivering with outrage. Michele half expected the other woman to proclaim, "You aren't the boss of me!" But Michele stood her ground and stared her down. It wasn't long before Britney took her seat again, and Andrew slunk to sit contritely next to her.

"We have a mission," Michele reminded the Las Vegas Purists. "Not only do we have to eliminate our targets, we need to do it in such a way that we don't get caught."

"I'm not afraid of vampires," Andrew spoke up.

"I am," Michele told him. "And if you're not, then you must be suicidal. The vampires are going to suspect that hunters have targeted them. That war's been going on for centuries, and we are prepared to continue the fight. What we need is a way to keep the human police from looking for us. It is important that we not be suspected by our own kind."

"We act in secret," Britney said, with a flare of rebellion. "We know that."

"Then help me think of a way to cover our tracks."

"Why worry about it?" Britney gestured toward the television. "The cops can't even catch this gang of thieves."

Michele turned her attention to the TV screen. After watching the news anchor's report on the increasing intensity of a local crime wave, she turned back to her fellow vampire hunters.

She smiled. "Britney, my dear," she said. "You are brilliant."

"Okay," Pete said, "your turn."

Phillipa took a sip of ice water while she concentrated on the word game they were playing. "Umm . . . The only thing that comes to mind is *CSI: Hogwarts*."

Pete laughed, and nodded. "Good one."

"No, it's easy and obvious, but you're sweet."

"Hey, I'm trying to make a good impression on you." He reached across the small table to touch her shoulder. "Am I?"

She almost shied away, fighting the odd notion that Pete didn't have a right to touch her. She made herself smile at him. "You don't have to impress me."

Phillipa looked around the hotel bar where they'd been sitting for the last couple of hours. She had the feeling she was being watched, but she didn't see anyone looking her way. This wasn't the first time recently that her brain had played tricks on her. "I'm on too many drugs," she muttered.

"Is that a confession?" her cop friend asked.

"Just a fact I'm trying to learn to live with. I'm still a rookie at managing this whole thing. I'm sure eventually it'll all become SOP."

She found it odd that while she had trouble discussing the subject with everyone else, she didn't have any problem talking about it with Pete. Was this trust because she was attracted to him as more than a friend, or because she had no emotional investment in him at all? She'd had a good time with him in the five or six hours since they'd left the church, but if she decided to go up to her room right now, she wouldn't be inviting Pete to come with her.

Which was good, right? Taking it slow was good. Normal. She wanted normal.

I want Bridger.

She ignored the voice in her head, even though the longing was like some primal animal inside her trying to claw its way out. She couldn't spare the time or energy for this confused passion crap.

She looked at her watch. "Excuse me," she said, and took a black zip bag out of her purse. "You don't mind blood, do you?"

"Well, actually —"

"Don't worry, I won't bleed in front of you."

Phillipa understood his squeamishness, but she was also learning to make the things she had to do just another part of daily life, as she'd been advised. She unzipped the bag and arranged the necessary equipment on her lap. When she pricked the side of her finger, she was careful to keep her hand below the level of the table while she touched the blood drop to the testing strip. After a five-second wait, a number appeared on the monitor's small screen.

"Ninety-three," she said.

"Is that good?"

"Better than it should be, considering what I had for dinner." She'd been *starving,* with far more appetite than she'd had in months. She'd feared she'd overindulged, but the numbers told her otherwise. "Maybe Vegas agrees with me. I've been pretty normal since I got here."

There was that word again: normal.

"What is so important about being normal? Are you all right?" Suddenly Bridger was seated in the chair beside her, holding her hand. "You're bleeding."

"I *was* bleeding," she said, knowing full well that the pinpoint stab wound had drawn only a drop of blood. She tried to tug her hand free. "How's Octavia?" she added, and was immediately annoyed with herself for blurting that out.

"I wouldn't know," Bridger said. "She went home with Jason." His expression went from worried to bemused. "That incident happened after you left — you must be reading my mind. Memory. Whatever." He grinned. "You're jealous."

Bridger's dimples were astonishing. Almost as much as his arrogance. Though there was something about the way he kept thrusting himself into her presence that she found . . . overwhelmingly sexy, if not actually charming. And she wasn't going to deny that she was jealous of Octavia, no matter how embarrassing that was. Maybe it wasn't jealousy, so much as —

"Who the hell are you?" Pete demanded. "And do you want to let go of the lady's hand?"

"I do not," Bridger answered, not even glancing Pete's way.

He kissed her hand. More precisely, he pressed his lips against the spot where she'd drawn blood. It was somehow . . . intimate. Exciting.

"Weird," she said, and forced herself to take a steadying breath. "Pete, this is Matthias." She gave Bridger a stern look. "He's

119

just leaving."

Bridger's gaze bored into her; and she could have sworn that his eyes held a faint gold glow, like a wild animal staring hungrily out of the dark. That look ate her alive, and left her shaken when he turned away.

"Good evening," he said as he stood. "Nice meeting you, Pete."

Phillipa's hands were shaking, so she clutched them together tightly in her lap as he walked away. Had she said something to her sister about liking dangerous men? Well, that was just plain nuts.

"Who was that guy?" Pete asked.

My worst nightmare. My wet dream come true.

"Just some jerk relative of my brother-in-law's," she answered her nice, normal friend.

She had to fight hard against the impulse to follow the jerk and have her way with him in the middle of the hotel lobby.

She concentrated hard on the other man. "Tell me about this case you've been working on."

"Everyone in the city and county's working on it," he answered, leaning forward eagerly. "And the Feds have come in on the case as well. All the casinos are beefing up their security, so this is a good time if you're

120

really interested in going into the private sector."

"Never mind me right now." She waved a hand. "So this is big enough to form a task force?" He nodded. "Tell me about the case."

"We've got a crew, maybe more than one crew, of very high-tech robbers."

"This is just a robbery investigation?"

"Just? Woman, remember where you are. This town lives, breathes, and eats money."

"Has anyone been hurt? Killed?"

He shook his head. "That's likely only a matter of time, but the civilians in the banks, casinos, and residences this crew has hit have been lucky so far."

"Banks, casinos, *and* home robberies? Are you sure this is a crew of pros?"

"I know it's unusual for robbers to be so diversified in their targets. That's one of the reasons the investigation is so tough. We haven't been able to pinpoint patterns of where they might hit, or when. It doesn't help that they're using electronic equipment that screws up not only surveillance cameras, but also witness's memories. And the victims are all cooperative, even docile, during the robberies."

"What?" Phillipa was both confused and outraged. "How is that possible?"

He shrugged. "All we have so far is theories. Maybe they're using some sort of aerosol drug to gas the witnesses. But no residues been found at the crime scenes, or in blood tests on the victims."

"Audio wave technology?" Phillipa suggested. "Like the sort of thing cruise ships have used to scare off pirates? It makes people disoriented, doesn't it?"

"That's being looked into," Pete told her. "But you'd think getting blasted with noise would leave people with headaches instead of fuzzy memories."

Phillipa yawned, then apologized.

"You're tired." Pete looked concerned. "How do you feel?"

As legitimate and caring as the question was, it still grated. She forced a smile. "Fine. But I *am* tired. I think it's time I went to bed."

He stood and put his arm around her shoulders to escort her out of the bar. At the elevator, after the briefest brush of her lips across his cheek, she got on alone.

Chapter Twelve

"I'm leaving tomorrow," Matt said.

"Fine," Phillipa answered. "Have a nice trip."

She'd known who it was even before she answered the knock. She'd known she shouldn't have opened the door, especially since all she was wearing was a short black silk nightgown. And sure enough, there Matt Bridger stood in the hallway, looking all disheveled and manly in his shirtsleeves and with his collar undone.

He looked her up and down like he was ready to eat her, but what he said in his sexy British accent was, "You're being rude."

"I am," she agreed. The hotel was overly air-conditioned, yet the air around her was full of heat. She could barely breathe for it, but she managed to add, "I don't know why."

He moved forward and blocked the door with his shoulder when she tried to close it on him. "You're going to miss me when I'm gone."

He was right, and maybe that was why she was being so bitchy toward him, hoping that would protect her from the pain.

"You're stalking me," she told him when he kicked the door closed. "I don't find that attractive in a man."

"You do in me."

"Oh, please —"

He took her by the shoulders, pulled her to him, and kissed her hard. Her toes curled tightly against the thick carpet, and she clutched at his back, overwhelmed by sensation, desperate for more.

Kissing him was like riding a hurricane! And that was just kissing. Sex was —

"Oh, hell!" she snarled, pulling away from the enticement of his mouth. "You drive me crazy!"

"*I* drive *you* crazy? Woman, I'm not the one whose blood —"

"What?"

"Never mind." He let her go. "I know I shouldn't be here."

A wave of fear went through her. "What *are* you doing here? I didn't tell you my room number. Did you follow me?"

"I'm not stalking you — any more than you are me."

"I've been trying to avoid you."

"Really?" He raised a skeptical eyebrow. "Have you been able to stop thinking about me?"

"That's none of your bloody business."

"Let's not talk about blood — and why's a Yank girl swearing in British?"

"I lived in London for a year. Not that that is any of your business, and I don't know why I'm telling you."

"Because —"

Matt shook his head. He could explain it to her. He could tell her that they needed to know about each other, to share with each other, to *be* with each other. He owed her the explanation, but to say it out loud meant he'd have to acknowledge the reality of their attachment as well. How could he walk away then? And if he didn't walk away —

"I shouldn't have come."

"No." She proved that her will was stronger than his when she gestured toward the door. "Go."

He slowly turned from her and took a step, then another. Her hand landed on his shoulder before he could take a third.

"Stay."

He stiffened. "Are you sure?"

"Yes. No. Yes. Damn it! I hate all this melodrama."

He turned his head, and couldn't help but smile at her annoyed expression. "Why?"

"For one thing, stress plays hell with my blood sugar."

"I see."

It was her turn to smile. "You haven't the faintest idea what I'm talking about, do you?"

Her features lit when she smiled, but there was sadness in her, and a bit of desperation in her eyes. He came closer to her, the need to be with her driven by concern this time. She tensed, and he knew that she wanted his touch, but need warred with prickly pride.

"What are you hiding from me?"

"I'm not hiding anything. It's just none of your business."

She was completely correct, and also totally wrong. He coaxed her, "If I tell you one of my secrets, will you tell me yours?"

A hint of humor replaced the dread in her eyes. "You have secrets?"

"Deep and terrible ones."

She couldn't fight her curiosity. "Oh, yeah? Like what?"

Matt gave a careful look around the room, then leaned close to her and whispered, "I enjoy watching figure skating."

She laughed, and smacked him on the shoulder. "You fiend!"

"There's worse," he promised her. "But now it's your turn."

Phillipa knew it would come to this. She also knew that this fear of showing weakness and imperfection to Bridger was stupid. Maybe it was best to tell him and get it over with. If it scared him off, that would be a good thing. He would give her an excuse to hate him once he was gone.

"I'm waiting," he said.

"I have diabetes."

There. She'd said it.

He looked puzzled.

"Adult onset, but type one, insulin dependent," she added, even though she was sure that meant nothing to him. You had to be part of the club to understand the private language. He stepped back, which was pretty much what she'd expected him to do. "It's not a contagious disease," she pointed out.

"Someone in my unit was diagnosed with it when I was in the service," he said slowly. "He received a medical discharge."

"That happens a lot with diabetes," she answered between gritted teeth. "Though not as often as it used to."

"It happened to you," he guessed.

She shrugged. "I'm on medical leave, but I don't know if I'll ever be a street cop again."

"Diabetes causes you to have too much sugar in your blood, yes?" He smiled.

"It makes you die if it isn't treated properly," she snapped.

He ran a finger along his jawline, and she heard the faint scratch of stubble. "So that's what Marc has been up to."

This was not what she'd expected him to say. "Huh?"

"Of course that also explains why you're so sweet. My cousin knows I have a terrible sweet tooth." He smiled, and his teeth seemed awfully sharp. "All the better to —"

"You're making no sense, Bridger." In fact, she wished she hadn't changed her mind about wanting him to stay. He had no clue what talking about the disease to him cost her. "And you're pissing me off."

He chuckled. "Such romantic language you use."

Then he took her face between his hands, and kissed her gently on the forehead, and on each cheek. The warmth of his touch soothed her, and set her tingling.

When his lips brushed across hers, she distinctly heard him say, *It doesn't make you*

weak. It doesn't make you damaged. It just
makes you sweeter to me, even though he
couldn't possibly be speaking.

It didn't make any sense, but his reassurance was a balm to her frayed senses
and self-confidence.

Wait a minute.

If anyone was going to restore her sense
of self-worth, it was going to be her. Having
some sexy male tell her she was all right
wasn't what was going to make it so.

But it still felt good.

She didn't want him to ever stop touching
her, or to stop holding her like this.

But he was leaving tomorrow.

She had a moment of being completely
miserable, but fought it off. "I can live
without you," she said.

"But you don't want to."

"Which is a stupid thing to say."

"For both of us."

She'd been having these disjointed conver-
sations for several days now, and was beginning to hate it. "I just don't get it," she said.
"I mean, here I stand in my nightgown, half
naked —"

"I noticed."

"— talking like an idiot to a man I barely
know who sounds just as idiotic as I do. Do
you know what's going on?"

"I'm afraid I do."

"Then explain it to me!" she shouted.

"We're trying not to fall in love," he said.

Too late, she thought, but said, "We're not in love. Lust, definitely, but —"

"Do you want an explanation or an argument?"

She wasn't sure what she wanted, other than him in her bed for as long as he wanted to stay. And wasn't that pathetic? Especially when she knew already how much it hurt when he went away.

"And what do you mean, *so that's what Marc's been up to?*" she demanded, suddenly remembering his earlier comment.

"Matchmaking." He took a seat on the edge of the turned-down bed. "Marc thinks I should take care of you."

"I can take care of —"

"Of course, your sister has demanded that I stay away from you."

It wasn't like Jo to interfere with her life. "Why?" she questioned. Indignation knotted in her stomach. "Because I'm sick?"

He shook his head. "Because I'm a hard man."

She gave a quick glance to his crotch. "Really? I mean —"

He laughed. "Woman, you know exactly what I mean. Your sister is correct. Being

130

with me wouldn't be safe for you."

I need safe. I need normal.

For all that this was true, the voice in her head was mocking. She wanted adventure. She wanted this man with his dangerous edge. Not that he'd done anything dangerous since they'd met; it was just this feeling she had when she was around him. Electrified. Excited.

She wanted —

"Melodrama," she complained.

"I know." He sighed. "I come from a people who thrive on the stuff." He shook a finger at her. "You could get addicted to it, you know."

"I don't need an addiction. Not with all the drugs I'm already on."

He looked her over with a careful, critical eye. "Tell me, sweet, just how much medication are you taking?"

Why did she get the feeling he meant it literally when he called her "sweet"?

"Insulin four times a day," she told him. "Pills for my blood pressure, for my heart, for my kidneys, for depression." She forced a grim smile. "Shall I go on?"

"Bloody hell." He shook his head. He looked more indignant than sorry for her, which she appreciated. "How did this happen to you?"

"I got shot."

"With what? A voodoo curse?"

That seemed as good an explanation as any the doctors gave her. "A few weeks ago, a suspect shot me in the arm. When they patched me up, a whole lot of tests were run and I was told my body was burning itself out because my autoimmune system was crashing, and that I was about a month away from dying from a disease I didn't know I had."

"Leaving your life and career in shambles," he concluded.

"Precisely."

She noticed that the thin straps of her nightgown had fallen down over her shoulders. She supposed this made her look all wanton and ready, and wondered why she felt excited rather than embarrassed.

"Is that the worst secret you've got? That you are ill? Do you think that's enough to drive me away from your bed?"

"Well — yeah."

"Were you diabetic last night?"

"Yes. But —"

"Did you have the disease the first time we were together?"

She remembered how she'd been thirsty all the time back then, which was one of the symptoms. "Probably."

132

"If it didn't kill us then, I doubt it will kill us now." He held a hand out to her. "Come here."

CHAPTER THIRTEEN

While she stared at him as though she'd been struck by lightning, Matt carefully assessed Phillipa with all of his senses. He could tell that what was wrong with her was serious by the way she acted. He had no experience with illness, but it was easy enough to see how it could affect pride, sense of worth, even identity.

He could detect a great many artificial substances coursing through her blood and muscles. Perhaps he had not detected drugs before because their purpose was to keep her body's functions in balance. The same science that allowed him to walk in the sunlight helped control her serious human disease.

"Modern medicine is amazing," he murmured. "But not as amazing as you look in that nightie. Come here and let me take it off you." When she still hesitated, he rose to his feet. "Or I could come fetch you."

"Yes, you could," she said, but came toward him anyway, her walk and lilting smile equally seductive. She pressed her hands against his chest when he reached for her. "Ground rules."

He was close enough to be enveloped by her warmth and her scent. "Enough talking, woman."

"Almost." She began to unfasten his shirt. Her fingertips trailed heat along his skin as she slowly bared his chest. "This time we're going to have rules."

He'd been having trouble thinking through the growing sensation, but now he grew wary. "Why?"

"You're going home tomorrow."

Any vampire could tell you that home was where your bondmate was. "I am going back to England."

He couldn't think now why it was so important for him not to bond, but he was sure it would come back to him once he was away from tempting, lovely, enticing Phillipa.

He put his hands on her hips and drew her closer. "This is no time for conversation." He caressed the sleek skin beneath the fine silk.

She'd finished opening his shirt by now, and ran her hands down his chest and stomach. "We're negotiating."

"I don't believe in negotiating." He stroked a thumb up the inside of her thigh.

Her voice caught on a gasp, then she went on. "We're going to have lots of hot sex, without the melodrama."

"How can one have hot — ?"

"Passion isn't the same as melodrama."

"Really?"

He twirled her around and onto the bed, and came down bedside her. The nightgown had fallen down to her waist, leaving her breasts bare. He kissed her throat, and ran a slightly extended fang across the tender skin. He could feel the blood racing beneath her flesh. She pulled his head up before he could go any further.

"Talk to me, Bridger."

Desire was demanding his attention, but he managed to focus enough to look into her eyes. "Lovely eyes." He covered her breast with his hand. The nipple was hard against his palm. "What do you want to discuss?" he asked when she arched against him.

"Don't stop," she said as he caressed her.

"I don't intend to."

"And don't walk out this time."

He sat up and turned away from her.

"I thought you weren't going to stop."

He stared across the room to where partially opened curtains showed the garish lights of the city below. Danger roamed somewhere outside this room, beyond this momentary safe haven.

"I can't stay," he said, though desire demanded otherwise.

Before he could turn back to her, she knelt behind him and put her hands on his shoulders. "Of course you can't stay." Her voice was tight with the effort to remain even, to keep her words practical. "You have a plane to catch. You have a life to go back to."

Maybe a wife and kids at home.

He started to deny her thought, but let it go. Let her believe whatever she had to.

"Stay with me tonight," she said.

And though she could have hidden it from a human, he was aware of her desperation. He shared it.

"I'll stay with you tonight," Phillipa went on. "We'll behave like adults this one last time. Nobody walks out on anyone. Deal?" She gave a low chuckle that cost her dearly though it didn't sound forced. "I'll even give you a ride to the airport. Deal?" she asked again.

Her fingers kneaded the tense muscles of his shoulders. He rolled his head, enjoying the moment, forcing dread of tomorrow from his mind. He shouldn't have come to her at all, but the scent of her blood back in the bar had been too strong to resist. He had tried fighting the want for nearly an hour, an hour that had only made the need for her stronger.

Sex, but no blood, he negotiated with himself. Not a drop. Not a taste.

The thirst burned through his being, but he couldn't risk tasting her again. They were already too close to bonding. He'd prayed he'd never feel this compulsion for the blending of souls that made a Prime complete.

I need you, he thought. In more ways than you'll ever know.

There's only one way you have to need me right now.

She shared his thoughts!

He wanted her to share his blood.

His life.

But that kind of selfishness could get her killed.

Tonight they would share each other's bodies, and that would have to be enough.

"One last night," he whispered.

Phillipa ran her hands down Matt's back, memorizing the feel of his body, seeing him by touch as she kept her eyes closed. She wanted her memories of him to be strong, and as sensory as possible.

When he turned to her, she knew instinctively that he wanted to possess more than just her body, but was holding himself back, trying to keep emotionally distant, to just fuck. She told herself she could bear it, but she couldn't.

"No!" She buried her nails deep into his shoulders and dragged him down on top of her. "Make love to me. *Me!*"

"You can't und—"

I can take it. I can take anything you have to give.

His gaze met hers, green eyes full of intense hunger. There was a threat of violence in the hard line of his mouth. A long moment passed where Phillipa couldn't breathe. Fear raced through her, intensifying the heat zinging between them. Then he smiled, and the sight of those deep dimples melted away every sensation but deep, insistent longing.

"You'll be sorry in the morning," he told her.

"Then I'll worry about it tomorrow." And prayed that morning would never come.

He gave a short, sharp nod. "All right, then."

She caught the glitter of sharp white teeth. Then his mouth came down on her throat, and the strongest orgasm she'd ever known took her. Yet, even as she soared with it, she knew this was only the beginning.

CHAPTER FOURTEEN

Why am I howling?

The thought flitted into his mind as his voice rang eerily out across the desert once more. He caught hold of the words and hung onto them for dear life.

Words.

He looked down at his paws, and licked an itching spot on his foreleg where the dark fur was matted and covered with sand. He stood up and shook a lot of dirt and grit off himself. He didn't like being dirty.

I understand words.

He listened carefully, his ears swiveling to take in every nearby sound from this hilltop. He was utterly alone now, his cries having scared off every creature within a couple of miles.

I know what a mile is.

Why was I howling?

Loneliness.

Calling for the pack.

Why am I alone?
I.

He blinked, trying to see the world through different eyes.

Okay, I've got that now. I am. I am — who?

He lifted his head and howled again.

Stop that! Someone will hear.

That's the point of howling.

Yeah, but I don't want to get shot.

Try again.

I am —

He panted with the effort, but made himself think. Like a man. It was so hard it made his head hurt, and the pain made him want to stop and go back to just being.

It's not bad being a wolf.

That's a man thought. Do another.

He was thirsty. He'd been baying so much his throat ached. The sun would be up soon. He needed shelter. The day would be hot. He might be seen. What place is this? Why will the day be hot?

I'm in the desert. That's bad. I'm closer to an arctic wolf than to a desert —

I'm not a wolf.

Not a man, either.

Man. Wolf. Shape. Shape . . . something . . .

Shape-shifter.

Werewolf.

That's me. He sat down on his haunches.

That's good to know.

What did it mean?

His jaws cracked wide in a yawn. Thinking was tiring. He knew he had been asleep, but not because he'd wanted it. Something — someone — had sent him down into a long, dark sleep. He growled at knowing someone had done something to him.

He ached all over, his head hurting the worst. Maybe he could think more, better, after he rested.

Rising, he turned around slowly, taking in his surroundings. There were plenty of boulders, and deep cracks in the hillside rocks. He moved toward one deep opening, but the scent of long-ago death put him off making his den in the most suitable spot. He picked a large boulder and padded toward it. It would offer him shade from the coming sun, and concealment as well. He dug out a shallow hole so he could squeeze farther under the rock, then settled into the depression. Sleep came instantly.

He knelt beside the blond woman. She was scratched and bloody and naked, but she looked at him with defiance, even as the wildness left her bright blue eyes. He wished she hadn't morphed back to her human shape; it was harder for him to kill a woman.

"Hi," he said. He shouldn't talk to her. He

should just do his job. "What's your name?"

"Do you really want to know?" his companion asked. "Considering . . ."

"You're going to kill me," the woman said. Her gaze never wavered from his. She lifted her head proudly, exposing her throat. "Go ahead. I don't want to live like this."

In that moment, he knew he couldn't do it. It wasn't her fault the mad bastard had attacked her and turned her. She hadn't killed anyone yet. How could he punish her for a crime that wasn't her own?

"It's not bad being a werewolf," he told her. "Not after you learn to control it."

She was skeptical. "Control the change? How?"

"It's a matter of technique, and practice, and a strong will."

"Can you teach me?"

"You look stubborn enough to survive."

"I can't go on like this."

"Then I'll teach you."

"Isn't that breaking your own laws?" his friend asked.

"Bending them," he admitted. Sometimes you had to bend the rules. "You haven't told me your name," he said to the woman.

"Cathy," she answered. "What's yours?"

"Mike."

Michael Bleythin.

He woke up with the memory of his name. And the knowledge that he knew how to morph, that he'd been born knowing. And that he had a friend, a partner named Matt. And he had a pack. Cathy was one of them, back home in San Diego.

He still didn't quite remember where he was, or why, but he knew the information was locked in his brain, buried under what had been done to him. He'd figure it out.

Then he would hunt.

But he couldn't hunt until he was human again; not if he had to go into the city. His enemies frequently retreated to the cities, didn't they? Cities disguised scent. Cities were a place to feel safely surrounded by those who didn't really believe that werewolves were dark creatures that sprang forth out of the night.

Which was always a cool thing to do.

But first he had to morph from black wolf back to Mike Bleythin.

He stood and stretched and arched his back. He glanced at the pale blue of the early-morning sky and breathed deeply, taking in the scents, faint from the past and sharp with the present, that made up the distinct perfume of his surroundings. His senses were sharp in human form, but not this sharp. He always missed being in wolf

145

form, but right now being in man shape was a necessity.

Yet for the life of him, he couldn't remember how to do it.

He knew it wasn't something he normally thought about, it was something he just *did*. Morphing was an act that flowed through the muscles and sinews and bones.

Only now it wouldn't.

For a moment, it frightened him to near panic. Was he crazy? Maybe he was a wolf who thought he was human. Or maybe he was a man having a hallucination that he was a wolf.

Maybe he was just chasing his tail.

And that was what the vampire wanted.

He growled, remembering that it had been a very psychic vampire that had messed with his mind, causing him to be this way.

When anger helped the panic subside, he found that he was pacing back and forth across the hilltop. Stupid move, to be out in the open like that. What kind of green pup was he, to let himself be silhouetted on high ground in broad daylight?

He made himself sit back down beside the boulder and tried to think. For a while he was distracted by the scent of a rodent cautiously stirring a little ways away. It made him want to hunt, and it made him hungry.

His wolf self came up with a simple strategy to pounce on the poor little mouse, but his human self took control again before he could proceed with the hunt.

Once again he tried to make the change back to human, and once again he failed.

The effort left him in pain and panting. The noise of his ragged breathing caught the rodent's attention, and it fled. He wasn't going to panic again, or mourn a missed breakfast.

What he wanted was — his pack.

Yes. But the pack wasn't anywhere near. He couldn't very well make his way all the way back to San Diego in his current form. He had an image of trying to hitchhike by standing next to a highway and sticking out a paw. If this was a Disney movie or a credit card commercial, that might work, but in reality he was more likely to get shot, or run over by a truck.

If he couldn't get back to his pack, what was he going to do?

Then he remembered the dream. Not only did he have a pack, he had a partner. The vampire had assumed he was in town working the case with his partner. That wasn't true, but his partner — Matt — Matt was in town, wasn't he? He was one of too many vampires that had showed up in Vegas for some party, right? Matt and all his vampire relatives' presence had gotten in the way of Mike's case.

But . . . what was his case?

The vampire must have blocked that information, along with the knowledge of how to morph. *One crisis at a time. One step at a time.* First, he'd find Matt.

Mike started down the hill, toward the city. He had to find Matt. And he hoped to the Moon that Bridger was still in town.

The problem was staying inconspicuous. In the daylight. In Las Vegas. There were plenty of predators in town, but he was the only wolf in wolf's clothing out on the morning streets. He was a big guy, six foot three, over two hundred pounds. He had the same mass in either form, so he was a pretty damned big wolf, not likely to be mistaken for a malamute on steroids.

His little brother Joe always wore a chain with a gold medallion engraved with his name and phone number. That way, when he was morphed, he looked liked he *belonged* to someone. This helped keep people from being scared at the sight of him, preventing the shoot-first-ask-questions-later syndrome humans had to anything that threatened their top spot on the food chain.

Mike had always scoffed at Joe's ID tag, teased the kid about being a good doggie. Now, as he moved with great care through alleys and back lots, he understood just how useful Joe's gold medallion was for undercover work in wolf form.

Every now and then he'd duck behind a Dumpster or the cover of a parked truck and try once more to regain human form. It never worked. And it hurt. The blazing headache from these episodes did nothing to help him hang on to sentience. The sensory assault wasn't doing him any good, either. There was nothing simple about the sights and sounds, or scents and textures, associated with human habitation. Because his brain kept trying to think more like a wolf than a werewolf, he knew that he was more sensitive and nervous because of the chaos than normal. It didn't help his mood that the day was growing hot, and he was covered in a heavy double coating of black fur.

Black absorbs heat, he thought grumpily as he moved silently along the back of a building, staying close to the wall. Even though he was in the shadows, the surface of the alley was hot beneath his paws. *Why couldn't I have been born into one of the white wolf packs? Of course, I'd still be hot, stuck in this shape in the desert.*

He was so intent on cataloging his own miseries that for a while he didn't recognize the almost subliminal buzz as more than just another irritation. But by the time he reached the street at the end of the alley, a word for the mental buzzing surfaced.

Vampire.

Somewhere nearby was a vampire.

Mike came to a halt. He kept part of his attention on the traffic pattern of the street he had to cross, and concentrated the rest of his senses on finding the other supernatural creature. There was more than one vampire, he decided after a few seconds. He picked up three distinct vampire auras, and he thought their energy was overshadowing and shielding the presence of one of his own kind.

If there was a werewolf with the vampires, what were the odds that he'd found the pair that had attacked him? And what was he going to do about it?

Investigate, of course, the man part of him told the growling wolf. *That's what detectives do. And put your hackles down, you look silly.* Or at least scary, and scary was not a good way to look while out on the humans streets.

Mike concentrated some more, and finally

150

decided on the direction he needed to take. He turned right and began to run. There was no cover to be had along the sidewalk, but there weren't any pedestrians nearby, and he could move fast. When he reached the corner, he had to leap over a car turning into the street, but he got across safely and ignored the car horns honking behind him. He heard sirens as police cars roared up the street.

The moment he hit the other side of the street, he saw that he'd inserted himself into an already developing situation. He skidded to a halt as three people walked calmly out of the building just ahead. Mike saw them more with a psychic vision attuned to detecting energy than with his eyes, and what his extra senses registered were two vampires and a werewolf. One of the vampires carried a large metal case. They were all wearing dark ski masks.

Vampires involved in a bank robbery? That made less than no sense.

The werewolf looked his way, and their gazes met. The werewolf took off his mask and bared his teeth in a way that signaled unmistakable challenge to their kind.

Mike finally recalled what had brought him to Las Vegas. He was hunting a murderer. And it looked like he'd found him.

Mike couldn't help but growl, and start forward.

Then a trio of police cars screeched to a halt in front of the building, lights and sirens adding to his sensory overload. Officers in Kevlar vests jumped out of the cars, guns drawn. A security guard came rushing out of the building doorway.

Matt's going to be really interested in this, Mike thought.

Then he noticed that one of the cops had a gun pointed at him.

If I live long enough to tell him.

CHAPTER FIFTEEN

Why am I doing this?

Michele Darabont had a plan to set in motion, but she couldn't remember how she'd gotten here. She stared blankly out the van's tinted windshield as the afternoon sun beat down on the busy street. The air-conditioning blew cool air into her face, and the others bickered in the back. She felt plucked out of her own life and set down in some strange movie scenario.

She gasped, and a shudder went through her as though she was coming awake from a nightmare. She tried to grasp what she'd been thinking, feeling, but she couldn't catch hold of what had been bothering her.

Which was just as well. She needed to concentrate, now that they were parked outside the vampire's lair; what they were about to do was highly risky.

Besides Andrew and Britney, they'd added

three more Purist fanatics to help carry out the op.

"All right, listen up," she said, turning in the driver's seat to address her troops. "I want you all to think about the consequences of what we're doing very carefully. We're the first hunters to strike a blow against the monsters for a very long time."

"It's long past time!" Britney chimed in.

"We're bringing the fight back to them." One of the others grinned maniacally.

"They'll bring the fight back to us if they find out hunters have done the killing," Michele warned. "This action isn't sanctioned by our side."

"Who needs the so-called *official* vampire hunters?" Britney demanded. "We're the only legitimate hunters. We actually *hunt* vampires."

There were murmurs of agreement from the others.

"Let's get it on!" someone shouted.

"The point is, this has to remain a secret op," Michele went doggedly on. She was trying to give something of a reverse pep talk to the group, and they so obviously didn't want to hear it. "We're breaking a treaty."

"One that should never have existed," Britney asserted.

"I agree. But we all have to accept the threat that hangs over our heads for this. We'll be hunted by the vampires, and by our own kind, if we are identified. Today we're striking a blow for what we know is right. With luck, we'll spark a reaction from the monsters that will bring the rest of the hunters back into the fight."

"You've been through this before," Andrew complained. "We know what we're risking."

Michele sighed. She didn't think they did, but she let it go. "Let's execute the plan — get in, do the job, get out. Right?"

"Right!" they answered in unison.

We're all going to die. "Let's go," she said, and reached for the door handle. "We have a lot of equipment to unload." *What the hell am I doing here?*

"Okay, what you do is purl one row, then on the next row you need to knit two, then slip one knit-wise, knit one, do a yarn over, then pass the slipped stitch over the knit stitch *and* the yarn over."

"You realize that I have absolutely no idea what you just said," Jo told her.

Phillipa smiled at her sister. "I knew you were going to say that. How many times have I taught you how to knit?"

155

Jo laughed. "The same number of times that I have forgotten. You know, I've always thought it was sweet, in a weird way, that a tough street cop likes to knit as a hobby."

Phillipa gestured at the framed tour T-shirts that lined one wall of the room. "It's no weirder than your collecting Def Leppard memorabilia."

Jo smiled fondly. "Marc gave me those."

"Excuse me? I know I gave you the one from the *Hysteria* tour."

"But I lost it, and Marc replaced —"

"How? When?"

"During that wildfire I got caught in out in the desert, when Marc and I met."

"You've always been a little sketchy about how you met."

Jo totally ignored her curiosity. "Show me how to do that stitch again."

Phillipa was perfectly content to do just that, and their needles clicked in contented silence for a few minutes.

They sat close together on the couch in the Cages' living room, finally sharing some quiet sisterly domesticity. Brandon was sleeping in a carrier set on the low coffee table in front of the couch, looking all sweet and warm and peaceful. A huge flat-panel television set was playing across the room, muted for the sleeping baby's sake. Some workers in white coveralls were on a metal scaffolding suspended from the roof outside the condo, washing the wide penthouse window, but otherwise Phillipa and Jo were alone.

"Wasn't it nice of Dad and Mom to take the Cages off your hands and fly them back to their respective homes?" Phillipa asked.

"Very nice," Jo agreed. "And now you're going to stay in the guest bedroom, right?"

"Don't you two want some privacy?"

"I didn't say we were going to be here, did I? Marc needs to get back to New York tomorrow to cater some red-carpet thing."

"I thought he was supervising the food at some red-carpet thing here."

"He is, but that's tonight. So we're heading out in the morning. You can stay here as long as you'd like."

Jo gave her a hopeful look. "Or maybe you'll want to move in with your friend Pete? It might not be good for you to be alone."

"Are you talking about monitoring my blood sugar, or something else?" Phillipa asked suspiciously. She had no intention of moving in with Pete, or any other man. How could she, after . . . "Damn," she muttered.

"You were with him last night, weren't you?"

Phillipa couldn't pretend her sister was talking about Pete. "Yeah, I was with Matt," she answered. "But don't worry about it; I left him at the airport before I came here. He's long gone from my life."

Except that she could still feel his hands on her, and taste his mouth — but the memory wouldn't be so sharp with the passing of time. She should hope it would, but she didn't.

"Unless his flight was delayed," Jo grumbled. She glanced briefly toward the window washers. "Those guys must be new at the job. They're awfully jumpy."

"*Jumpy* might not be a good term to use," Phillipa told her empathic sister. "Considering that they're hanging on the outside of a very tall building." She gave the workers a quick glance, but the sight made her uncomfortable, so she turned firmly away. "That's definitely not a job I'm going to be applying for."

"I think it might be fun. Lots of fresh air. Nice views."

"Daredevil. You survived a plane crash and went right back to work."

Jo gave another fond, dreamy, sloppy-in-love smile. "That's because Marc convinced me to give it a try. I didn't think I'd ever want to fly again, but he knew I needed to."

"I'm going to throw up any second now." Phillipa looked at her watch. "Or at least demand that you feed me lunch. If my blood glucose wasn't starting to get low from hunger, your syrupy adoration of the big fellow might send me into a coma."

"I love the guy. Hey, what's that?" Jo's attention was suddenly on the television. "Is that a wolf?"

Phillipa looked toward the screen as Jo picked up the remote and turned up the sound. The picture on the screen was in grainy black and white, and tilted at an odd angle, but Phillipa could make out a huge dog amid the chaos.

"This footage of the attempt to halt the bank robbery, shot several hours ago, is from a traffic camera on the street corner," the announcer said. "The animal accompanying the robbers was shot, but it and the robbers somehow managed to elude capture by the police."

"How?" Phillipa looked at all the police vehicles and officers within the restricted view of the camera. "The perps are being swarmed by cops, and —"

Her words were cut off by a loud crash, Phillipa jumped to her feet as a huge section of plate glass shattered into the living room.

The workmen leaped off the scaffolding and poured into the room. Still dressed in white coveralls, they now wore black ski masks over their heads.

Michele's last orders to her people had been a firm, "Make it look like a robbery. Leave the sister alive. We want a witness."

She realized this command might be impossible to carry out, when the sister plunged a metal knitting needle through Kevin's arm as he rushed toward the whore.

He screamed, blood spurted, the baby began to cry, and the sister planted herself squarely in front of the real objects of the attack.

Then Britney came at the woman from the side, tackled her around the waist, and brought her down.

CHAPTER SIXTEEN

He really was going to get on the next flight. Bridger fed more quarters into the slot machine next to his boarding gate. McCarran Airport was set up like any Strip casino, only the theme here was the hustle and tumult of a very busy international airport.

He'd won and lost the same twenty dollars for several hours now. He alternated between feeding the slot machine and watching the huge screens that advertised the hotels' glamorous shows, comedians, and magic acts. Whenever an ad cycled through featuring a certain magician, Bridger's attention returned to the slots.

It was a way to pass the time between the flights to London that he kept not getting on. He hadn't been able to bring himself to step onto two planes so far, and the airline people were getting rather annoyed with him. Being telepathic, he was able to soothe their irritation, and dispel any fears that he might be some sort of terrorist.

He let them think he was a gambling addict who couldn't pry himself away from gaming, when the addiction he was fighting went much deeper than that. He kept having visions of what life could be like.

"Bugger," he muttered.

He really should leave, no matter how much the bonding need called to him. He couldn't recall if he'd shared his blood with Phillipa last night, but he was still drunk with the taste of her. He could do the right thing and get as far away from her as possible, or he could do the easy thing and go to her and claim her as his own.

So far he hadn't yielded to temptation. But he hadn't managed to leave Las Vegas yet, either.

I'll take the next flight, he promised himself.

Only to have the promise instantly forgotten as fear stabbed through him, followed by a swift rush of anger. Neither emotion was his own, but they belonged to him — as she belonged to him.

"Phillipa!"

She was in trouble. He started running to her aid.

And vampires could run very fast.

■ ■ ■ ■

Phillipa went down when the intruder tackled her. She turned the attack to her advantage by going down on one knee, then rolled across her attacker and back onto her feet. The masked attacker was now on the floor, and Phillipa kicked him to keep him there.

A quick look showed her that two of the intruders were intent on ransacking the condo. But two more were closing in on Jo. Jo had snatched up Brandon and was backing toward the center of the living room.

"This way!" Phillipa pointed toward the exit. Jo's gaze flicked to her, and she gave a quick nod.

One of the intruders shoved something at Jo. Phillipa wasn't sure it if was a gun, but she kicked at the outstretched hand. Jo used the diversion to dash toward the hallway, and Phillipa followed hard on her heels. They reached the door and were out of the condo within seconds. Phillipa slammed the door behind them just in time, as the crack of a bullet ricocheting off the closed door reverberated out in the hall.

"Damn!" Phillipa snarled. She grabbed Jo's arm and pulled her toward the elevator.

"Let's go!"

Jo ran beside her, but gave a fierce look back. "They could have hurt the baby!"

Phillipa had never heard her sister sound so angry. "It's not wise to mess with a mother."

"Damn right." Jo clutched the wailing Brandon closer to her chest.

"Don't worry," Phillipa told her. "They're here to rob the place. They won't come after us."

Then the door flew open behind them, and she knew she was wrong. Well, crap. This was not the way a B&E normally went down.

The sound of the gunshot behind them was deafening, and the bullet left a dent in the copper elevator door before ricocheting into a wall. The shooter fired again. This time the bullet hit the elevator's call panel, shattering it just as Phillipa was getting ready to press the Down button.

She didn't know if this guy was deliberately trying to trap them, or if a wild shot had done it for him.

"Not good," she breathed.

"Stairs," Jo said, and led her to a door around a corner. "Hold him."

Phillipa took the baby and watched their backs as Jo punched numbers into a keypad.

The door lock clicked open, and they ducked through into a stairwell. Their attackers reached the door before it was fully closed, but Jo gave a mighty tug, getting it closed and locked again before the others could follow them inside. Then she snatched her son back from Phillipa.

"This is the emergency exit down to the garage." She started down the stairs. "Hurry up!"

Phillipa looked down the stairs, and closed her eyes for a moment. She couldn't remember how many stories the penthouse was above street level, but she knew racing downstairs wasn't going to do her any good. But there was nothing for it, not when they had the baby to worry about. She wished she'd had lunch, or at least been able to grab her purse before having to flee.

"Too late to worry about it now," she muttered, and hurried after Jo.

"Damn!" Michele swore. She turned on Andrew. "Why did you shoot out the elevator controls?"

"I was aiming for the brat," he answered.

"Can you shoot the lock off this door?" Kevin asked. Blood soaked the sleeve of his white coverall, and he was holding his injured arm close to his side. "Are you sure we can't kill the sister?" he added.

"I agree," Britney said.

"She was protecting her family," Andrew spoke up. "She doesn't understand that they're the enemy."

"For somebody who isn't the enemy, she's done a hell of a lot of damage," Britney complained.

"What about the lock?" Michele asked.

"Everybody stand back."

The Purists backed away from Andrew as he took careful aim at the keypad.

"Freight elevator," Michele said before he took a shot.

They'd used the freight elevator to gain access to the roof. She quickly led them back to the condo entrance. Even though she dreaded climbing onto the scaffolding again, this was the fastest way to catch up with their quarry. You did what was necessary for the cause.

Phillipa stopped as they reached the bottom landing to take long, deep breaths. She had to get it together. She was used to being a little dizzy sometimes, and sometimes a little nauseated. It was par for the course, and all that crap. Only right now she felt really nauseated, and really dizzy, and the world was kind of fuzzy on the edges of her vision.

She reached into her pants pocket, and found it was empty. She usually carried a roll of glucose tablets with her, but she'd been so upset about Bridger's departure this morning that she'd forgotten just about everything else.

"What now?" she asked. She was the big sister, the cop, she should be taking the lead. But it was getting harder to think by the second. "Sorry," she said, and began to weep.

Jo turned to her. "This door leads to the parking lot. We can use the OnStar in my Jeep to call nine-one-one."

"Clever."

"If you hang with the Cages, you learn a few survival tricks."

Why? Phillipa wondered, but she was starting to shake, and it would take too much energy to ask. Jo pressed buttons on another keypad, and Phillipa followed her into the building's underground parking garage.

Where figures in white coveralls were waiting for them.

CHAPTER SEVENTEEN

The alarm that went off when Matt broke down the door to the garage was silent to human ears, but the subsonic whine was sharply painful to his. The pain merely fueled his desperate anger: *nothing* would stop him from getting to Phillipa.

He ran down a short flight of stairs, and as he went through an open doorway, a bullet struck the doorframe, then zinged across his cheek. Hot pain seared in a line across his face, but he ignored it, and the gunman. Instinct demanded he find Phillipa; that was all that mattered.

The garage was filled with rows of cars and supported by thick concrete pillars. He was aware of the presence of at least eight mortals lurking there, most of them hunters. Two were being hunted. One was bawling his lungs out, which was not aiding his mother's effort to hide.

Bastards! How dare they hunt a child!

Matt needed to get to Phillipa, but protecting the baby came first. As he dashed toward the sound of crying, a low moan came from behind a concrete pillar to his right, and a gunman stepped out of cover to point his weapon squarely at Matt's chest.

"Look out!" Phillipa shouted, staggering out from her hiding place.

Matt turned toward her, heard the gunman squeezing the trigger . . .

"Oh, no, you don't," a deep voice rumbled. And Marcus Cage streaked across the garage to knock the shooter to the ground.

Dealing with one vampire was hard enough, but two monsters was not a scenario they were set up for. They hadn't really thought one would ever appear.

"Withdraw!" Michele shouted to her team. She feared she was about to lose Andrew to the murderous fury of his attacker.

But the monster hadn't finished off Andrew just yet. He kicked the gun far across the concrete floor, where it disappeared under a car. Then he ran straight for where his human whore cowered with her brat.

Michele waved her people toward the nearest exit, praying the distraction would last long enough for them all to get out. The others moved quickly, unnoticed by the monsters, but she wasn't so lucky. The first vampire stalked toward her, all fangs and claws, with fury burning in his glowing eyes. Her blood ran cold with terror, and her mind froze as well. Michele Darabont knew she was going to die.

Then the other woman appeared, and stumbled a few steps toward the vampire before sinking to her knees. The vampire's attention was immediately on the woman. As he ran to her, Michele went to Andrew.

"He'll kill her," Andrew rasped as he struggled to sit up.

"Better her than us." She helped her groggy henchman to his feet, and they ran for their lives.

Matt knelt beside Phillipa as the Cages came running up.

"What did they do to her?" Marc asked.

Matt gathered Phillipa into his arms. She was very pale, her skin clammy. "I don't know. There's no blood."

Her life was fading, and he couldn't bear it. He couldn't think for his own pain.

Josephine thrust the baby into Marc's arms and dropped down beside him. She felt Phillipa's forehead, and said, "This has to be hypoglycemia."

"What's that?" Marcus asked.

"Her blood sugar's way too low, low enough to make her pass out. If it gets too low, it could kill her. We have to get her to the hospital."

There was something wrong with Phillipa's blood? Relief flooded Matt. "I can help her. I can share my blood —"

"No!" Josephine declared. "She's needs a shot of glucagons or a glucose IV. Not —"

"She needs my blood."

Marc knelt beside him and put a hand on his shoulder. "Not unless you're willing to make a permanent commitment, my friend. Do you take this woman —"

"No!" Matt shouted, rising to his feet with Phillipa in his arms. "I can't do that to her."

But he could feel her fading. He had to —

"We have to get her to a hospital," Josephine insisted. "Now!"

Her fierce shout brought him to his senses. Mortals could save her, in a mortal way. He had to accept that this was for the best, no matter what his instincts shouted at him. "Let's move."

"This way." Josephine led them toward a bright red SUV. Along the way she said, "Marc, honey, you smell like fish."

"Lobster," he answered. "I was at work

171

when I got your psychic scream for help."

Marcus's bondmate had called out to him, Matt realized. Just as the woman who should be his — could be his — he couldn't *risk* being his — had called to him. It was one more sign they were meant to be together.

"Damn it all to hell," he muttered, and got into the back of the SUV, gently cradling Phillipa on his lap. "Drive," he ordered. "Hurry."

This sucks.

Mike crawled deeper behind the row of garbage cans and licked at the drying blood on his flank. At least the bleeding had stopped.

And it hurts.

I hate being a werewolf.

No, what he hated more than anything right now was humans. Was it any wonder that sometimes his kind ate them? Wolves and men were never meant to be in such close proximity. There could be no trust between them, no friendship. Never mind all that "man's best friend" doggy-loyalty belief from humans, and the whole "we've got it good, the trained monkeys'll always feed us" attitude from dogs. Real wolves couldn't live around men. Men feared other predators, and men destroyed what they feared.

Take his situation, for example. He'd just been doing his job, saving the human world from a monster, and along comes a cop and shoots him! Just because he was there.

Looking like a huge, dangerous, snarling wolf.

Okay, maybe the cop had a sliver of a reason for what he did, but Mike was still wounded. He was still in pain, and he was still totally pissed off.

And he was hot, he was mercilessly thirsty, and the garbage he hid behind stank. Even worse, he still couldn't morph back to his more convenient human shape. He wasn't sure how bad his wound was, but it hadn't started to heal yet, which was not a good sign at all. Had the vampire managed to take that skill away from him as well?

Were the humans hunting him?

How was he going to find Matt like this?

Most importantly, was night ever going to fall so he could move through this cursed human habitation without the fear of being seen?

"Are you sure that's how the incident happened?" the police officer asked Marc.

Matt paused in his pacing around the ER

173

waiting room to watch as his cousin held the earnest young copper's gaze.

"That is exactly how it happened." Marc's deep voice was a gentle, firm rumble. The sort of voice one would believe even if Marc wasn't hypnotizing the man as he spoke.

One of the peskier parts of living semi-openly among mortals was the occasional need to convince the humans that supernatural beings didn't exist, and that there were logical explanations for even the most bizarre occurrences. Marc was trying to keep mortal authorities out of vampire business now. Let the mortal police think they had jurisdiction over bringing justice to the attackers, but vampires took care of their own.

Matthias Bridger defended the Families, and he concentrated on what he had to do while Marcus talked to the mortal cop. If he let himself think too much about Phillipa right now, he'd do more than pace, but it was better for her this way. Mortal medicine could control her disease.

But he could cure it.

He pushed the temptation away and stepped up to Marc as the officer walked away. "Now what?"

The other Prime turned to him, all the ferocity he was feeling showing only in his eyes. "We hunt."

Matt could still feel the limp weight of Phillipa in his arms, raising his rage again. "Good."

Josephine approached them before anything else could be discussed. Marc took Brandon from her, and held the baby easily against his broad shoulder. "How's your sister?"

"She's good," Josephine answered with a relieved smile. "She's stable and sleeping peacefully. The doctor says she can go home when she wakes up." Her expression clouded. "To the hotel, that is. We don't have a home right now. We have a crime scene."

Marc put his arm around his bondmate's shoulder. "We're all safe. Everything else is details."

She rubbed her head against his chest. "Yeah. But if they stole my T-shirts, they're going to be in big trouble."

Marcus's cell phone rang, and he returned Brandon to his mother's arms and flipped open the phone.

A nurse stepped up and tapped him on the shoulder before he could speak. "Take it outside, please."

Marc nodded and went out the nearby exit.

"Cell phones aren't allowed inside hospitals," Josephine explained when Matt gave her a puzzled look. She shook her head and leaned close to whisper, "The things your folk don't know about our kind could fill a vampire self-help book. Don't worry so much," the empathic woman added. "Pip's going to be fine."

"Pip?"

She put a finger to her lips. "And *I'm* going to be fine as long as you never tell her I called her that. That's what she was called when we were kids."

"I promise." He stored the nickname away, glad that Phillipa's sister seemed more kindly disposed toward him. "Can I see her?" he asked. "Since she's asleep, I promise —"

He stopped as Josephine's attention shifted over his shoulder. When he turned to look, he saw Pete Martin coming toward them. It took an effort not to snarl at the mortal.

"I came as soon as I heard about the break-in," Pete said. "How is she? Can I —"

"Heads up, people," Marc said, only a few steps behind the man. "We have to go now." *Octavia's called a meeting,* he added telepathically.

176

Octavia? Matt questioned.

She's the closest thing we have to a local matri. She's called in every vampire in town. Your presence is especially requested, cuz.

"Now," he said again, and took his bond-mate's arm when she looked like she was about to protest. "We'll come back for Phillipa when we're done." He looked into the mortal's eyes. "Pete'll stay with her, won't you?"

"Of course," Pete answered. "That's why I'm here."

Jealousy tore through Matt, but he fought to ignore it. He fought to ignore his own instincts. *This is best for her.* If he couldn't have her, he had to let her go to a mortal who would look after her.

But he still hated Pete Martin's guts.

"Let's go," he said, before he could change his mind.

CHAPTER EIGHTEEN

"Why not let the police handle it?" Jason Cage asked.

He was seated on one of the arms of the couch. All of the seven vampires, and the two mortal bondmates that lived in Las Vegas, were gathered in the living room of Octavia's home. Octavia sat in a wing-backed chair, looking as imperial as her name suggested. Marc and Josephine sat on the couch, the baby sleeping across Marc's lap.

Matt stood by the door with his arms crossed, waiting for the locals to have their say. Las Vegas was Family territory, but not a highly populated one, even though the Clans said they were welcome to it. Marc and his lady were part-time residents, as were several others here today. The city was a good place for business, but the psychic vibe wasn't appreciated by most vampires on a long-term basis.

"The police are already looking for this gang anyway," Jason went on. "They didn't know the home they invaded belonged to a vampire. There's no reason for us to take this personally."

"Are you crazy?" Nathaniel Strahan demanded.

"What happened to that hotheaded boy I arrested so long ago?" Matt murmured, almost to himself.

Jason gave him a bitter look. "I grew up." He looked at Nathaniel. "We protect our own, of course. But this wasn't an attack on the Families."

"These mortals attacked our women and children!" Anastasia was the city's other female vampire, and bonded to Nathaniel. The pair sat very close to each other on a piano bench. Nathaniel's arm was tightly around her waist.

Jason ran a hand through his thick brown hair and looked at the family on the couch. "I'm sorry if you think I sound uncaring. I'm not. But I learned the hard way not to interfere with mortals. There's no reason to return violence with violence in this case, since there's already a massive manhunt for this gang."

"What do you think?" Octavia questioned the other two local vampires.

"These people are getting a lot of media coverage," Micah Cage said. "We might not want to insert ourselves into a situation that's already so high-profile. It's not like we're Clan boys out to save the mortals from themselves."

"Jason has a point about this being a random attack," Elder Ross Waite said. He looked at Josephine. "Or does he?"

She looked thoughtful before she answered. "My sister is an experienced police officer. She thought we would be safe from the robbers once we escaped from the condo. They were wearing coveralls and masks and there was no way we could identify them, so there was no reason for them to come after us. But they did, and they shot at us. They followed us to the garage. No — they were waiting for us there."

"They ambushed you?" Octavia asked.

Josephine nodded. "They were trying to kill us."

"You're certain of this?"

After another thoughtful pause, Josephine nodded. "If it wasn't for Marc and Matt, they would have killed us."

"Perhaps we're dealing with vampire hunters," the elder said.

"Oh, come on," Jason protested. "They

180

don't do that anymore."

"There *is* a group of Purists in the area," Octavia said.

"The Purists have been robbing banks?" a skeptical Jason asked.

"A copycat diversion," Matt suggested. "The Purists could have disguised themselves as the robbery crew to draw attention from their own activities."

Jason stood and gave a scathing look around the room. "You all want a fight, don't you?"

"You are Prime," Ross said. "Don't you?"

"Not with mortals. Especially not with pathetic mortals like the Purists."

"They would have killed my mate and child," Marc rumbled angrily. "I want them dealt with."

"Of course," Jason said. "But don't count me in on this fight." He glanced at his watch, then nodded politely to Octavia. "Excuse me, but I have things to do."

She gestured toward the door. "Go feed your beasts, my dear. We'll deal with the mortals."

When Jason approached the door, Matt didn't get out of his way. Their gazes locked for one hostile moment, but then Matt reminded himself that his quarrel with Jason was in the past; he had current business to deal with. He moved aside to let the other Prime go.

With Jason gone, Matt moved forward and got everyone's attention. "I have jurisdiction here." He looked at their hostess. "If Lady Octavia so agrees."

"I ask for your help in the name of our community," she responded.

"As do I," Ross, the eldest among the Primes, added.

Matt nodded, then turned slowly to look at everyone in the room. "I will explain the rules of the hunt so that we are all perfectly clear. None of you will interfere with my actions. None of you will question my actions. You will give me any information and help I require. Understood?"

There were nods and murmurs of agreement, though not a single Prime looked happy with the rules Matt laid down. He didn't blame them, as the need to be in control was as much a part of being Prime as the cravings for blood and sex were. But at least no one argued with him. He used to relish the territorial disputes that ended with his drawing first blood from those who questioned his authority, but no longer. He must be getting old and jaded, because these days he preferred simply getting on with the job.

"They tried to kill my mate and child," Marc said. "Hunting them is *my* job."

And what of my mate? She's the one in the hospital. To Marc, Matt said, "As Brandon's guardian, I claim that my right to lead the hunt comes before yours."

Marc gently passed the baby to Josephine and got to his feet. "I've got to disagree with you on that, Matt."

"Marc, I don't want to fight you," Matt said as the bigger Prime approached.

Marc gave a crooked grin. "Because you think I'll win?"

Matt smirked. "Hell, no, because you still smell like fish."

CHAPTER NINETEEN

The concrete was rough and cold beneath her hands and knees. Phillipa didn't understand why that bothered her more than anything else, when the whole world was shutting down around her. Cold concrete was the only thing that seemed real. In the distance there was shouting, and shooting, and a baby crying. She knew she should open her eyes, because somebody needed to do something heroic, and it was up to her. But opening her eyes would only make the dizziness worse, and then she'd throw up. There was nothing heroic about vomit. Cold sweat rolled off her, and the shaking was getting worse.

Somehow she got to her feet and forced her eyes open. That was when she saw the vampire. Her vision was fuzzy, and it was as if she was peering down a long, darkening tunnel, but at the end of the tunnel she could clearly see a vampire standing there. Though it was shaped like a man, long fangs sprouted from its mouth and claws warped the shape of its hands. And its eyes were glowing an angry, fierce yellow.

"Matt?"

You do realize that this is a hypoglycemia-induced nightmare, right?

Right, she agreed with the sensible part of her subconscious.

"Matt?" was still the first thing she said as she woke up.

"He's not here."

The baritone voice was familiar. It was warm, and nice. She'd never have a dream about *him* being a vampire.

She turned her head and opened her eyes. She wasn't surprised to find out that she was in a hospital room, or to see him seated by the bed. "Hi, Pete."

He put down the magazine he'd been reading. "Do you want me to call him?"

"Of course not." Her heart said differently, but her heart was no more reliable than any other part of her body. "He left for England today." She sat up slowly, and smiled tentatively at her friend. "It *is* still today, right?"

He glanced at his watch. "You were brought to the emergency room four hours ago. You've been napping."

185

She yawned and rubbed the back of her neck. "I haven't gotten a lot of sleep the last few nights." She felt herself blush, and saw that Pete noticed. She cleared her throat. Then she gasped as memory rushed back. "Jo! Brandon! Are they all right?" She swung her legs off the side of the bed.

Pete grabbed her shoulders as she started to stand. "They're fine. Stay where you are." He gave her shoulders an affectionate squeeze before taking his seat again. She watched his expression change from friendly concern to the neutrality of an investigator. "What happened?"

Phillipa gathered her thoughts, then calmly recited every detail of the incident, up to the point where her blood glucose crashed and she thought she saw a vampire in the basement.

"I really don't know what happened after we reached the garage," she told Detective Martin. "Do you?"

He checked a small notebook. "According to the statements from your sister and brother-in-law, Mr. Cage arrived home at the same time that officers arrived on scene. The perps had disabled all of the building's security cameras, but they missed one of the alarm systems."

She vividly remembered being chased and

shot at, and for a moment she was as scared as any civilian in the same situation, but it passed into professional calm. "They were apprehended, right?"

Pete shook his head. "Not yet."

Phillipa swore, and slapped a fist down on the mattress. "What is *with* these guys? We were watching the news about them robbing a bank when they broke into Jo's place. Busy little bees, aren't they?"

"Too busy," he answered. "That's why I'm thinking your home invasion might have been a copycat crew."

"Why? These guys do burglary as well as armed robbery, don't they?"

"But two jobs in one day is not their pattern. At least it hasn't been." He flipped the notebook shut. "And they haven't shot at anyone before, either."

When I'm done with them, they won't shoot at anyone ever again, she vowed. Nobody attacks my family and gets away with it.

But she kept these vigilante thoughts to herself.

"They weren't wearing the masks when they first showed up outside. So maybe they thought we could recognize them, to come after us like that," she told Pete.

Did that mean that the threat might not

be over? That her little sister and nephew were still at risk?

"Could you ID any of them?"

She closed her eyes and tried to bring up details of the group that had been on the scaffolding. "There were five of them, in white coveralls. One was tall and skinny. There was a blond — long hair tied back. At least one was female."

"You saw that while they were still outside?"

She shook her head. "When we were fighting. Girls feel different than boys, you know."

Pete smiled and nodded. "I have noticed that. This helps," he added. "Anything else?"

"I stuck one of them with a knitting needle," she told him. Ha — now Jo couldn't tell her that her hobby wasn't suitable for a tough street cop. "It was a wooden needle. If he'd been a vampire, it would have killed him."

Pete looked thoroughly puzzled. "Except that there aren't any vampires."

"It was a joke." Why had she said that? It wasn't just because of the dream. Something else nagged at the back of her mind, something important. She couldn't force the information to surface, though; it would come in its own time.

"Anything more? Could you work with a sketch artist?"

Before she could answer, Jo peered around the edge of the doorway. "How are you doing? Can I come in?" She stepped inside and held out Phillipa's large leather purse. "I brought your stuff."

Phillipa took the bag and dumped the contents out on the bed beside her. "Everything's here," she said. "My testing equipment, insulin and sharps, pills."

"What about your wallet?" Pete asked.

"Yeah, that's here too. Pretty inefficient thieves," she said as she flipped through the wallet and found cash and credit cards undisturbed.

"We don't think they took anything from the condo, either," Jo said. "Marc and I did a walk-through and couldn't find anything missing."

"They let you back into the crime scene?" Phillipa asked. "Why'd you go back there?"

"Can I have a minute with my sister?" Jo asked Pete.

"Sure. I'll get some coffee. Can you have coffee, Phillipa?"

"I can. And I'd love some."

"None for me, thanks," Jo said when he looked questioningly at her. She waited until Pete was gone before she said, "Would you mind if I left town? More importantly, do you think you'd be all right here? Or would it be better if you came with us? And thanks for saving me and the baby, Sis. If you hadn't gotten us out of there . . ."

Phillipa was aware that her fast-talking sister was both guilty and sheepish. And probably still in shock from the earlier danger.

"You're the one who got us out," Phillipa told her. "I only got us as far as the elevators. Then I passed out," she added grimly.

Jo hugged her. "You could have died."

"Yeah, and it was my own fault. If I'd had some candy on me we'd have made it to your Jeep without the added melodrama. And what do you mean, is it all right if you leave town? Of course it's all right. I'm not an invalid." Even if she *was* sitting in a hospital room. "It's not like you have a house to go back to, and you were leaving tomorrow anyway. Right? Marc has business to get back to."

"Yes. But he's very angry about the attack, and practically had to be beaten into seeing sense about leaving."

Phillipa laughed at the notion of her sister beating up on the big fella. "Apparently you won."

Jo grinned. "It wasn't me. It was more of

190

a family decision, and Marc agreed it'll be better if he takes me and Brandon home. But I'm not going anywhere unless I know you're going to be all right. You can come to New York with us. Or go home to Phoenix if —"

"I'm staying right here." Frankly, Phillipa thought it would be better if her sister and her family weren't in Las Vegas while she made absolutely sure the town was safe for them. "I've got job interviews, remember?" she reminded Jo.

"And Pete," Jo added hopefully.

"What about Pete?" Pete asked, returning with a steaming coffee cup in each hand.

"I've been hoping you'll have a nice romance with my sister," Jo said unabashedly.

"Hey!" Phillipa complained.

"I'm willing," Pete answered. "In fact, I'm actually here to ask your sister for a date."

Phillipa almost spilled the hot coffee, but managed to put it down on the bedside table. She stood up.

"That's great," Jo said brightly. "I hope you two have a good time."

"Excuse me." Phillipa waved. "I'm right here." She looked at her friend. "What are you talking about, Peter Martin?"

"Are you feeling well enough to stand?"

191

Jo interrupted.

Phillipa couldn't bear to be coddled, but there was also no way to lie to her empathic sister.

"I'm hungry, that's all. But I can fix that right now," she said, and plucked an energy bar from the pile of things she'd spilled from her purse. "Two carbohydrate exchanges, and I'll be just fine." After swallowing a couple of bites of the cranberry oatmeal bar, she turned her attention to Pete once more. "So — a date, Detective?"

"Sort of, Officer. I have to go see a man about a wolf, and I thought you might want to come along."

That sounded intriguing. Phillipa liked Pete a lot, and she welcomed any chance to get her mind off of Bridger. She also wasn't done discussing the attack with him yet.

"Okay," she said. "Let me do whatever I have to do to get out of here, and then we'll go see about a wolf." She smiled at her sister. "And you take your family to New York. It is okay if the Cages leave Las Vegas, isn't it?" she asked Pete.

"As long as the department knows how to get hold of them, that's fine." He came forward to help as she started stuffing things back into her purse. "As soon as you're done here, I'll take you back to your hotel.

You need to change into something nice to go on *this* wolf hunt."

CHAPTER TWENTY

Mike knew he was being hunted. The other werewolf knew he was trapped in this form, and that he was wounded. This would be the perfect opportunity to track him down — to track the Tracker. Wouldn't that be a coup of a kill?

It was dark now. Finally. And the torturous heat had faded. It had been the longest day of his life. Thirst and hunger and pain still nagged at him, but at least he now had the darkness to cover his movements.

And move he must. But where?

When the day started, he'd been confident of locating Matt somewhere in the city. Now he wanted to head back into the desert, to go to ground far from the danger and confusion and sheer terror that came from being in the midst of humans. In his current state, he could almost sympathize with why the lycanthrope killed them. To rid the world of humans would be a blessing. Or at least, escaping them would be.

That was the wolf part of him fighting the human part for dominance.

Enough thinking, Mike thought, and carefully got to his feet. The wound had stopped bleeding hours ago, and he slowly eased some weight onto his right rear paw. He damned near howled in agony when he took a step, but silence was as imperative as moving. He had to be a ghost, a shadow — even if a limping one.

Mike ignored the pain and slinked up the alley. He had to get out of here before they found him.

They?

He listened very carefully. The distant static of police radios caught his attention, and he made out the sounds of distinct car engines circling the nearby streets. His subconscious must have been aware of the pattern for some time, but now the sentient part of his awareness figured it out.

There was no doubt that the lycanthrope was looking for him. But so were the cops.

"Congratulations on your cleverness," the vampire said, taking a seat opposite Michele. Even coming from a monster, the sarcasm grated.

Michele didn't offer any excuses. "We

didn't get the brat or the bitch, but you don't have to rub it in. Next time —"

"I'm not sure there will be a next time."

Michele glanced toward the entrance of the restaurant. The rest of the Purists were due to meet her here at any moment. They wouldn't react well to having a vampire in the same room with them, even if this one was a sort of ally.

"This isn't a good time to talk," she told the vampire.

"I quite agree. But since I have pressing duties to attend to, now will have to do."

Well, the sooner she was away from the vampire, the better. This superior, supercilious creature made her skin crawl. She'd never reacted so strongly to one of its kind before. She didn't know if she was more repulsed by what it was, or attracted to the psychic power it exuded.

She knew it wanted her to look it in the eyes, but she fought the urge to obey. "Do you have information I can use?"

"Your targets are leaving town," the vampire answered.

Michele swore. "When? Is there any way we can get at them?"

The vampire gestured dismissively. "Don't worry about them. Let's discuss the problem you caused me with your clever little charade."

This time Michele couldn't help staring at the vampire. "What are you talking about?"

With her gaze caught, all she could do was listen.

"I am talking about your crew disguising yourselves as my crew. Your place in my scheme, little human, is to draw my kind's attention away from *my* activities. I set you on the child to focus the Family on hunting down an old, convenient enemy. But what do you do? You draw their attention to the very thing I'm trying to divert them from." The vampire *tsk*ed. "I'm very unhappy about that."

Fear rippled through Michele, and she felt the vampire tightening its mental control over her, letting her know how easy it was for it to make her its puppet. This creature had no regard for the agreed-upon rules vampires had observed in the last century about how they used their powers. Not all of them could exert this sort of mind control, but this one —

"Yes, I am unique," the vampire boasted. "And I have grown bored with being good. I've decided I want to be very, very rich, so I've been taking what I want from the mortals. I have nothing to fear from their law enforcement, but I knew that it was only a matter of time before my own kind would start noticing the psychic nature of the crimes. So I set you up as a diversion for our own law enforcement. Then you showed up at the Cages' disguised as my crew. I am very angry you did that, but I have managed to salvage the situation."

The creature reached across the table to squeeze Michele's wrist. The only reason Michele didn't scream was because the vampire wouldn't let her.

"I have a friend who would like to eat you," the vampire said. "If I didn't still think I could use you, I would let him. The Cages are leaving, but I have another assignment for you."

"Another diversion," Michele managed to grate out.

"Just so." The vampire's attention flicked away from Michele for a moment as one of the Purists arrived and took a seat at the table. The vampire smiled at him. "Hello, Andrew."

He smiled back, and looked into the vampire's eyes. "Hi."

"There's something I want you to do for me," the vampire told him. "I want you to kill Phillipa Elliot."

His gaze still locked into the vampire's, Andrew smiled more widely. "Okay."

■ ■ ■ ■

"Now I know what Octavia meant," Matt told Jason Cage.

He'd come up close behind the younger vampire, who was projecting a silence that affected every living thing in the backstage space, vampire and animal alike.

Jason didn't react to Matt's sudden presence but continued to project calm. There were quite a few caged animals in the area, including a pair of wolves lying in the shadows by the room's back wall, big cats mostly. Some of the animals were roaming free; Jason's hand was on the head of a white tiger, and the animal was leaning against him, looking up adoringly.

Jason wore tight black trousers tucked into high boots and a black velvet vest decorated with embroidery and jewels, but no shirt. A modern stage magician's costume, Matt supposed.

Jason continued petting the tiger as Matt went on. "When Octavia said, 'Go feed your beasts,' I didn't think she meant it literally."

"Why not?" Jason asked. He glanced sideways at Matt. "The sneaking up is a nice trick, by the way, especially if George and Gracie didn't detect you." The wolves' heads lifted at what must be their names. "But you don't need to show off for me."

Matt shrugged. "Keeping in practice. Besides, there was a sign at the door saying no unauthorized persons allowed."

Jason gestured at the animals. "There's a good reason for that. I wouldn't want my babies getting into trouble because some stupid human walked in here and got slashed to ribbons."

"That *would* be a shame. I'm happy to see that your sympathy isn't with the humans."

"Why would it be?" Jason turned to face him, very much a Prime ready for a fight. Behind him, the tiger began to pace.

"Tuck your fangs in, lad." Matt held his hands up before him. "Do you have time to take me on right now?"

"Aren't you a little old for Prime games?" Jason shot back.

Matt chuckled. "No Prime ever outgrows this nonsense — we just come to realize that it *is* nonsense, even if we can't stop posturing. I'll even apologize for provoking you this time. You've heard from Octavia?"

"Yes, damn you." Jason closed his eyes for a second. He was calm when he looked at Matt again. "What do you want?"

Matt didn't mind that the other Prime was grudging, as long as he followed custom and was cooperative. "I detected a certain amount of sympathy toward the Purists from you."

Jason gave a harsh bark of laughter, causing the tiger to snarl. "I said they're pathetic — which is not the same as *sym*pathetic. I'm on stage in three minutes," he added.

"Tell me where to find them and I'll leave."

"Why would I know where — Cooperate," he grumbled, then sighed. "The only one I know about is a loser named Andrew. He showed up in the audience a couple of times and tried to disrupt the show. Having to keep him quiet and control the animals was a pain. He found out where I lived and tried to get my neighbors to drive a stake through my heart. So I moved, and took out a restraining order against him. It would have been easier to make him forget me — but you know I'm not allowed to do that sort of thing anymore."

"The details of your parole are not under my jurisdiction, mate. Where do I find this Andrew?"

"The last I heard, he works at one of the old casinos on Fremont Street. If you hang out there for a while I'm sure he'll find you. Will you leave now?"

"Gladly."

Matt turned, and before he took a step, he *knew.* Her presence was a heady perfume. "Phillipa," he whispered.

She was here. Nearby. In the theater. And she wasn't alone.

Why? The thought was mixed with both jealousy and need — to see her again. To claim her.

At least to see her one last time, if only from a distance.

Goddess, bonding made a male pathetic! Especially if the Prime tried to go all Clanstyle noble and fight the instinct.

But he also wondered what Phillipa's interest was in Jason Cage — and he intended to find out.

CHAPTER
TWENTY-ONE

"Your wolf expert is a magician?" Even as she asked, Phillipa realized the answer. "Of course, or why else would we be here?"

Pete grinned as he took the seat beside her. "Because this act is getting great buzz, so I thought we'd mix pleasure with business. I've been dying to see the Beast Master do his thing, and we can go backstage afterward."

Phillipa smiled back at him. Pete was trying to entertain her, and she appreciated the effort. "Thanks."

She had concerns about stage shows involving trained animals, though she was more worried about the animals being well treated than about tigers jumping into the audience. That scenario was a remote possibility, and she supposed it was the almost subconscious frisson of fear of what might happen that made this sort of show so popular. It was scary-fun, like riding a roller coaster, not nearly as adrenaline-charged as chasing a suspect down a dark alley.

I miss adrenaline. But she was going to have to adjust to living without it, like large helpings of pasta or —

Matthias Bridger?

Even thinking his name was like a knife twisting in her gut. It was as if she'd heard his voice whispering in her ear, and she couldn't help but look around, no matter how foolish she knew it was.

The theater seating rose in a wide half circle from the stage. The plush seats were upholstered in black velvet, the walls at back were draped in black velvet curtains, and the thick carpeting was also dark. The whole effect was cavelike and mysterious. An exotic tone of sensuality was added by the long-legged waitresses wearing little more than bright feathers and sequins as they moved along the wide aisles taking drink orders. The auditorium was rapidly filling up, and there was a lot of anticipation and excitement in the air.

"Looks like the place is SRO," she said.

Pete looked smug. "I called in a favor to get us into the performance."

She reached up to touch his cheek. He was such a nice, normal man, and she really was very touched. She could learn to live without adrenaline, right?

"Thank you. I appreciate this," she said.

For a moment, everything went red. When the world came back into focus, Phillipa was on her feet, and she was shaking with reaction she knew, from emotions not her own. Anger. Jealousy. Regret. Bitterness — they'd all blown through her in one painful instant, like being hit with a category-five hurricane.

Pete was standing beside her, his hand on her arm. "What's the matter? How can I help?"

She didn't want anyone but *him* touching her! She fought down the urge to shake off Pete's concerned touch and looked around, certain she was being watched. By a hurricane named Matthias.

"I'm fine, I'm fine." She gave a shaky laugh. "A little rattled, that's all." She was just imagining things.

"You've had a rough day."

Pete's sympathy grated against her nerves, but she made herself nod and let him help her back into her seat. As she sat, the house lights began to go down.

She was wearing red, a silky slip dress that emphasized the curve of her breasts and hips and showed off the toned muscles of her arms and back. Damn, but his Phillipa was beautiful. Matt stood in the back of the theater and watched her hungrily.

He had to let the mortal touch her, talk to her, comfort her. He had abrogated his rights, but he hated it. It hurt, too. It was stupid to stand here and watch, but he had to make sure she was all right.

Custom said it was wrong to fight the bonding urge, and he was quickly learning that custom was based on a biological and psychic imperative that was hard to resist. Custom also said the bond was a perfect thing, a beautiful completion.

Maybe.

But he'd witnessed the dark side of the bond, knew what threat it could hold over a Prime and his bonded, knew what devastation came with the loss of such perfect love. He'd watched the Prime who'd trained him fall apart after losing his human lover to a vengeance killing. He wouldn't leave Phillipa open to that sort of danger.

She'd already been attacked once, in the never-ending war between mortals and vampires, and he wouldn't leave until he was certain she was safe. He should be out hunting for this damned Andrew right now.

But Phillipa was here — probably only to watch the show — and Jason Cage had just come strutting out onto the stage. He'd stay near Phillipa a while longer, at least until the show was over.

She still felt like she was being watched, but she ignored the sensation to concentrate on what was going on on the stage. The first thing she noticed were the two wolves. They were lovely creatures, lithe and lean, and they didn't look the least bit tame.

The man they walked beside was amazingly similar to his dangerous pets. He was tall and broad-shouldered but whipcord lean, his sharp features dramatically enhanced by stage makeup. He was dressed in velvet and jewels, and in this totally unexpected setting it took her a moment to recognize him.

"Wait a minute," she whispered to Pete. "I know that guy. The Beast Master is one of Marc's innumerable cousins."

"His name's Cage," Pete whispered back. "I wondered if there was a connection."

"He was at the christening."

She didn't mention that when she'd last seen the Beast Master, he'd been trying to pick her up. Of course, that led her thoughts back to Matt Bridger and his possessive reaction to the come-on. She'd been annoyed at the time, but remembering it sent a shock of desire through her.

And just like that, all the pleasure went out of the evening. There was a hole inside of her because he wasn't with her. It hurt so badly, she was tempted to get on a plane to England to find him.

Get over him. She'd made her choice when she took him to her bed. She'd known he was going to leave; she had no excuse to feel sorry for herself. *Get on with your life. Watch the show.*

She really *did* try to pay attention, but watching the animals was more entertaining than any of the illusions the magician performed. The big cats were the show-pieces, going through their paces with no more direction than a look or gesture.

The wolves didn't take an active part in the performance, but they went everywhere with Cage, flanking him at all times. This only added to the Beast Master's strong aura of commanding alphahood, the sort of behavior guaranteed to make the women in the audience all hot and bothered. Phillipa recognized the blatant sensuality, but it didn't do a thing for her.

While she didn't exactly get bored, after a while her mind wandered off in other directions. There was something she needed to remember. Something had been said or done at the hospital that had almost brought up a memory. This memory was valuable. It was a clue, wasn't it? Some*thing*? Some*one*?

Bridger?

Stop thinking about him and get your mind on the case. This someone has something to do with the case, doesn't he? Okay, it's a he. Young and tall and — a nutjob.

One of the attackers had been tall, the one that had done all the shooting.

The memory of the conversation at the airport came rushing back to her.

"Let me help you. You're in danger. They haven't corrupted you yet, but it's only a matter of time. It's dangerous for me to be talking to you. I'm under orders not to approach, but it's wrong not to try to save the innocent. You're sister's already damned, and —"

"All right. That's it." Phillipa spun around to face the nut. *"What is the matter with you?"* she demanded. *"What about my sister?"*

"It's not really her fault, but she's beyond saving now. He made her what she is."

"Who?"

"The vampire."

She'd dreamed about Bridger being a vampire, hadn't she? It must have been her subconscious's way of connecting the nutjob to the attack. After all, if there was one thing she was bound to pay attention to, it

209

was any reference to Matt Bridger. But it was her *sister* who was in danger.

Had they attacked her sister because they really thought Jo was involved with vampires? Did they think Marcus was a vampire? Why? Because Brandon already had a tooth? That was a little odd, but no reason to try to kill a mother and baby. There *was* no reason for what they'd tried to do, and she was going to see that they were put away.

Her gut told her that the nut from the airport was involved. She was going to have to find this guy, and fast.

As applause began, she realized the show was over, and she joined the rest of the audience as they rose for a standing ovation. Pete looked at her, and she saw that he was grinning like a kid.

"Good show," she managed, though she had no memory of whatever the last spectacular trick had been.

"Great," Pete said. "Fantastic. Now let's go talk to Mr. Cage."

She suppressed a nagging worry that she might have to ask a few questions of another Mr. Cage. "Lead on," she said to the LVPD detective. She was anxious to get this over with, so she could get on with her own case.

Phillipa was always amazed at the places

the flash of a detective's badge could get you into. A headliner's dressing room was not the oddest place she'd been on police business, but it was certainly the most interesting. The Beast Master's quarters were bigger than her apartment, with a kitchenette and large seating area. A thick blue floral carpet covered the floor, and the ceiling was painted with clouds and gilded cherubs. Vases of flowers and stuffed animals were everywhere, gifts from fans, she supposed. She was still too new to Las Vegas not to be impressed by the glitz and glamour.

Jason Cage graciously waved them toward a pair of chairs, and Phillipa was not only impressed but disconcerted that he had brought his wolves into the dressing room with him. One of them was curled up on the couch. The other one lounged on the floor in the kitchen area, where it was ripping great balls of cotton fluff out of a stuffed white tiger.

When Cage noticed her looking nervously at the wolf, he said, "They wouldn't eat anyone I didn't tell them to. Actually, they're too spoiled to hunt for themselves, and they're three-quarters malamute, anyway."

She smiled wanly at this reassurance,

knowing that he was lying, the way she always knew suspects were lying. But what was he lying about? And what was he suspected of?

Nothing, she reminded herself. Your senses are all screwed up. Pete's here to interview him as an expert witness.

"It's nice to see you again, Phillipa," Cage added, with the typical lascivious Cage male glint in his bright blue eyes. She frowned at him, and he turned an intense look on Pete. "You're here about the robberies, aren't you? How can I be of help, Detective?"

Pete gestured toward the wolf sleeping on the couch. "Are you sure those don't eat people?"

"I know that these don't." Cage moved to sit on the couch, and the wolf put its head in his lap. "There are a lot of European folktales about wolves attacking people, but there's no documented evidence of those tales being true. A rabid wolf might be crazy enough to attack a human, but it's not something a normal wolf is likely to try."

"How about a trained wolf?" Phillipa asked. "Could a wolf be trained to attack a human?"

"Of course," Cage replied. "But trained wolves are known as dogs, and I don't think Detective Martin came here to ask me about dogs."

Phillipa bit her tongue at this reminder that she wasn't the one here to ask the questions, and restrained herself from snapping a retort at the Beast Master. "Sorry," she murmured to Pete.

Pete nodded, his attention focused on Cage. "The remains of several people have been found in the desert recently. The indications are that they've been murdered, but the bones also show evidence of being gnawed." Pete gave a faint laugh. "Somebody in the department suggested we look for a werewolf, but it's more likely that the murderer has a pet wolf or wolf mix that's been allowed to feed on the bodies of the victims."

"That's sick," Cage said.

"Serial killers are very sick people," Pete said. "We haven't had any luck searching for this killer. Then a wolf turned up when the robbers hit a bank this morning. The robbers got away and so did the animal, but we don't think it was taken with the robbers. The police and animal control are looking for the wolf."

"You want me to help with this wolf hunt?"

Pete nodded. "There's an underground trade in wolves as pets, and these people don't talk to outsiders. My guess is that you're in touch with that community. I'd appreciate any information you might be willing to share."

Cage rose to his feet and gestured toward the door. "I'll consider your requests," he said as Phillipa and Pete also rose. "But for now I'd suggest you go with the werewolf theory."

CHAPTER TWENTY-TWO

The Beast Master had been hiding something, Phillipa was certain. But she was beginning to think that maybe secretiveness was the norm when dealing with Cages. She didn't mention her suspicions to Pete, because — well, because the Cages were family and you didn't turn on family, no matter how peripheral the relationship, until you were sure they'd actually done something wrong.

Besides, Jason's attitude could just be because he preferred animals to humans and didn't want to see a wolf hunt started in the streets of Las Vegas.

"Ms. Elliot?"

Phillipa jumped, then looked at the man across the desk and tried to remember where the hell she was. This wasn't another doctor visit, was it? Then she remembered, and grimaced. This job interview was an irretrievable mess, the "Ms. Elliot" was a very bad sign; before her attention had completely slipped to thinking about the case, this HR guy had been calling her by her first name.

"How long was I gone?" she asked.

"I beg your pardon?" he asked, all bland politeness.

Phillipa smiled. "It's okay. I admit I was, well, let's call it daydreaming." And not even about Bridger, although she'd had some graphically erotic dreams about him last night. She stood. "I have no business being here. When I got up this morning, I thought I could do this interview, that I could be sensible and normal, but I can't. Not today."

I'm taking my life back.

"Ms. Elliot, I have no idea what you're talking about."

"I know."

She picked up the very large purse that contained her insulin, monitor, medicines, glucose, emergency numbers, and all the miscellaneous crap she now carried with her. It weighed a ton, but she wasn't going to let it weigh her down.

"Does your behavior have something to do with the diabetes?" he asked as she headed toward the door. "I appreciate your telling me up front about your condition, but —"

"Hell, no," she told the concerned and embarrassed young man. "I'm tired of trying to make the world seem *normal;* I'm a cop, and I need to fix things. I have to be a cop again."

Merely working for a security company wasn't enough for her; she knew that now. As she stepped out of the air-conditioned building, she was hit by a blast of bright light and heat. She needed a strategy. Where did one go looking for a nutcase, especially in a town like this, where pyramids, fantasy castles, and Italian palaces were part of the landscape?

They'd met at the airport, and she was certain he'd followed her there. Which meant he knew her car. And where would he know her car from? From the parking lot at Jo's condo, was the most likely answer. They'd staked the place out, of course.

And he had been driving . . .

Phillipa closed her eyes to better focus on the memory of the airport encounter. Bright white sunlight pressed against her closed lids, and hot wind scrubbed her cheeks.

White.

Yeah. He'd been driving a white van. She'd been annoyed that she hadn't been able to make out the plates. She was even more annoyed now, but remembering the nutjob's ride was something, at least. Every piece of a puzzle helped eventually.

Had there been a white van in the underground garage? Her memory was too shaky to know for sure. But maybe the crazy vampire hunters still had the building staked out.

She opened her eyes, completely energized. She had a place to go and a clue to follow.

"Let the hunt begin," she murmured, with the fierce determination she'd been missing for months.

It had been a while since the radio in the rental car had actually played any music. It was annoying enough for Matt to deal with American-style driving without having at least some soothing background noise.

"Would a bit of Led Zeppelin be too much to ask?" he complained.

The newsreader continuing on about wars and oil prices and environmental disasters while Matt cursed the fact that he hadn't figured out how to work the unfamiliar sound system. It seemed very odd to be hearing about the traumas of the real world while driving the busy streets of the least real city he'd ever encountered.

He wondered what his night-dwelling

ancestors would make of this place. Then he remembered that his great-grandmum in Bristol had been here on holiday once in the 1980s. She'd broken the bank at one of the casinos playing high-stakes poker, and he'd had to remonstrate with her in an official capacity about using psychic talent to influence the mortal world. She'd grudgingly donated her winnings to charity, and that had been the end of the matter. It was embarrassing when one's own family broke the rules.

Then again, he supposed it was inevitable to have trouble with family when most vampires were related one way or another. Even the most righteous and upstanding of Clan boys had wicked Tribe cousins somewhere along the line, though both sides would be loath to admit the relationship. Family vampires weren't so proud and picky. They were allied with the Clans, and took in Tribe members who agreed to reform their evil ways. And as a result, the Families had the largest population of any of the three vampire societies.

"In local news," the woman newscaster said, "authorities have just released a statement confirming another bank robbery. Also, an anonymous source has informed this station that yesterday's daring penthouse raid by the same criminals was at the home of celebrity chef Marcus Cage."

Not likely, luv. Matt snorted. *And a good thing, too, or I'd have to turn my attention to a gang best left to mortal police.*

But the mention of Marc's penthouse did give Matt an idea. It wouldn't hurt to return to the scene of the crime for a good, long, psychic look at the place. Maybe he'd pick up a trail from there.

He smiled and changed lanes.

"Let the hunt begin," he murmured.

"This is *my* hunt," Andrew said, pacing the living room of Britney's apartment. "I'm going alone."

"You can't," Britney protested. She jumped up from the couch to step in front of Andrew. "Hunters work in teams."

"It's tradition to hunt in groups," Andrew answered. "That's all."

"It's safer," Britney said.

Kevin rubbed his bandaged leg. "Well, I'm not up to it."

Michele listened and worried, but she didn't join in the discussion. She knew this was the right thing to do, but something nagged at her. Something wasn't right. It was like she was searching for a memory that didn't exist. And she didn't quite feel she was all here.

"It's not that I mind killing the blond bitch," Britney said. "I like the idea. I want in on it."

"But she's not one of them," Kevin protested.

"She stabbed you," Britney reminded him. "She fought me. She got in the way of our doing the right thing."

"We ought to out them," Kevin said. "All of them."

"I've tried that," Andrew said. "With the magician, remember? Nobody believed me. Killing them is the only way." He stepped around Britney and began pacing again. "Killing *her* is the only way."

"He has to do it," Michele finally said. "Leave him alone to do what must be done."

Britney turned on her. "You're our leader. You're supposed to be the sensible one. Do you want him to get killed?"

"Phillipa Elliot is as human as we are," Michele pointed out. She glanced at Kevin. "She was lucky."

"I have a gun," Andrew said. "She won't have a chance to fight me or stab me. I'll do it from a distance."

"He'll be fine," Michele soothed her people. "It's important that he act alone."

She was certain of this. Only — she wasn't

sure why Andrew's solo mission was so imperative.

"I want you to kill Phillipa Elliot."

That had been said to Andrew. Only Andrew.

Michele rose and sternly addressed the others. "Andrew acts alone."

Britney quivered with frustration, but eventually she nodded. "Fine. But where? When? What's the plan?"

"I have to find her first," Andrew answered. "I'll stake out the vampire's place first and see if she comes back there."

CHAPTER
TWENTY-THREE

He needed a drink.

The day was too hot. His vision was blurry. Sound was fading. The pain was bad, but it was the thirst that was driving Mike insane.

He hadn't caught the scent of any water that wasn't too near people. There were lawn sprinklers merrily shooting water only a block away, but the sound and scent of this false rain was torture — he didn't dare try to get to them.

He couldn't take the risk of capture by the mortals, no matter how parched he was. He had to keep going, reach the wilderness before the hunters could close in. He'd find water there, and a safe den.

Somehow.

The only thing that was still working properly was his nose, but even that was intermittent, because his attention span was fading in and out. Scent was all he had to lead him out of the city, the only thing he could trust to help him avoid detection.

He'd long ago identified the individual scents of the human hunters, but it was the inhuman things creeping up on him that frightened him.

There was a werewolf ahead of him, blocking his escape into the desert. Waiting for him. Laughing at him. Ready to close in for the kill, but savoring the wait.

Mike understood the savage anticipation, and he welcomed the fight if he couldn't find a way to avoid it. He had to believe he would win it. That was the only way an alpha could think.

Behind him was a vampire.

It was a vampire that had gotten him into this mess in the first place. He was aware of the vampire in much the same way animals could sense impending earthquakes; it was a disturbance in the Force.

But escaping the wave of psychic danger heading his way, avoiding the vampire, drove him closer in the direction of the werewolf.

Were they working together?

Of course, remember how they were together back at the body site? Remember how they were together at the bank job? That was when I was shot by the mortal. Damn, it's hard to keep my brain working!

Mortals, werewolves, vampires — what had he ever done to deserve this much unwanted attention from people out to kill him?

He held on to the thought that it was the vampire's fault. Step by limping step, as he forced himself to move, Mike grew more and more angry with the vampire. And it wasn't advisable to make a werewolf angry. He was so tempted to turn and attack, but he talked himself into waiting until he found a time and place where he'd have half a chance.

He paused when he sensed the vampire creeping closer. He leaned his weight against a wall, the stucco hot in the sunlight. The effort to concentrate drained him, but information was vital if he was going to survive.

He listened, he breathed, he bent all his own telepathic senses on gathering intel. Both the vampire and werewolf were male, he decided, and healthy. Too bad. The werewolf was the one he'd set out to hunt — he couldn't remember how long ago that was.

The vampire —

There was something familiar about the scent and psychic signature . . .

Matt?

That was wishful thinking. Matt wouldn't stalk him; he would walk right up and confront him.

Matt would help him.

Hadn't he set out to find Matt Bridger? He couldn't remember how long ago that hunt had started, either. Time didn't mean too much when in this form.

He had to keep going. He'd find out who the vampire was soon enough.

He finally made his way into a warehouse area, where the large parking lots were full of row upon row of parked semi trailers. He was near the airport, because the roar of airplane engines filled the air. So did the stench of jet fuel, masking all other scents. If he couldn't detect *them,* then he was as masked from them as he was going to get. This was as good a place to make a stand as any.

Mike looked around, trying to use his human intelligence as much as possible. The wounded animal simply wanted to stand and fight and get it over with. Since wolves were excellent strategists, this animal attitude was embarrassing, and counter to survival.

He saw a lifted door at the back of one of the trailers. It was the closest thing to high ground, and he forced his aching body to make the leap into the back of the truck. Once inside, he crouched behind a pallet of cardboard boxes to recover from the effort to get this far. At least he wasn't bleeding from the strain on the wound; fresh blood would pinpoint his position to the others.

For a few minutes all he did was wait, gather his waning strength, and listen. When one of his trackers finally came near enough, Mike bunched his muscles and leapt.

He hit the vampire square in the chest. That should have knocked the vampire to the ground, where Mike could go for the exposed throat or belly.

Instead, the vampire grabbed him by the scruff and threw him to the pavement.

"Got you!" he shouted. "Now let's see about your friend."

What?

Puzzlement was the last thing he was aware of as the world went totally dark.

CHAPTER
TWENTY-FOUR

If crime-scene tape had been put up at the site, it had already been removed. This left the exterior of the building looking bland and inconspicuous, for which Phillipa was grateful. She'd heard a news report on the radio on the way over, revealing that the Cages' condo had been hit by the robbers. She'd half expected to find the hounds of the media out in full cry, but the activity surrounding the building didn't look any different than usual. She drove around the block slowly once to make sure.

While she hadn't been subjected to the same sort of media attention Jo had to endure when she survived an airplane crash, Phillipa had had her own run-in with reporters after the shooting incident that curtailed her career. She'd found having a microphone stuck in her face infinitely more daunting than having a gun pointed at her. At least with an armed suspect she knew what to say. "Drop your weapon or I'll shoot" did not work with a reporter.

When she saw nothing but a few cars parked in the guest lot at the side of the building and a glass repair truck in the back, Phillipa decided that the place was a media-free zone for the moment.

She pulled into the guest parking area, rolled down her window, and switched off the engine. The air cooled by the air conditioner was instantly replaced by the dry heat of the desert. She found the heat pleasant, even though she'd been warned that extremes of temperature had debilitating effects on diabetics. Surely, just a few minutes of hot sunlight wouldn't hurt her.

Please check the diabetic rule book in case you feel you're in danger of having any fun, she thought, but with less resentment than usual.

She spent another few minutes scanning the area, looking for anomalies. When she finally determined that nothing and no one was out of the ordinary in the neighborhood, she finally got out of her car and approached the parking garage. She didn't have a security keycard to swipe through the reader, but she remembered the emergency number her sister had used the day before and pressed those buttons for entrance. The metal door slowly came up with an almost grudging groan.

The moment she slipped inside the garage, all her senses intensified. The feeling was odd, but she *knew* she wasn't alone. It wasn't just a keen awareness that someone else was in the garage — she was drawn toward the other. And then she knew.

She stepped forward into the cool shadows and called, "All right, Bridger, what are you doing here?"

He came around a pillar and faced her, arms crossed. He was wearing sunglasses. "What are *you* doing here?" he responded.

For some reason she expected to see him sprout fangs in this setting, but she shook off the memory of the dream. And fought off the urge to run to the man. Just looking at him stirred aching need in her, but this was no time to let lust get in the way.

"Didn't I drop you off at the airport?" she asked.

He shrugged and took a step closer. "I missed my flight."

His voice sent an electric charge through her. There was a dangerous edge in his tone, and nothing friendly in the way he was frowning. Instead of being intimidated, she wanted to eat him up.

"That's no excuse," she told him.

"I wasn't offering any. What are you doing here?" he demanded again. "Why aren't you somewhere safe?"

"I'm investigating an attempted homicide."

"You aren't a copper anymore," he said in a steely British growl.

Which only annoyed her. "And you are?"

Suddenly they were standing toe to toe in the wide aisle of the garage, and she had no idea how they'd crossed the intervening space. He wasn't really that much larger than her, but this close, he sure seemed like it.

"Yes," he said.

For a moment she couldn't recall the question.

"I am a cop, of sorts," he explained.

"Not in this jurisdiction."

He gave a thin, dangerous smile. "The world is my jurisdiction."

Matt was aware that he was telling Phillipa too much, but being near her rattled him enough to loosen his tongue, as well as arouse everything else in him. "It isn't safe here," he told her.

Phillipa glanced around. "Why? Do you think I might get run over by a truck?"

He put his hands on her shoulders and drew her closer. "Anything might happen."

Bridger's voice was so rich with sensual promise that it sent a shiver through her. She considered the surroundings and said, "Sweetie, I haven't made out in the back-seat of a car since I was a teenager."

His answering smile showed the deep creases of dimples. "It might be fun to relive your youth. In my youth we used carriages," he added.

She guessed that he was somewhere in his forties. "Britain wasn't that backward in the seventies. You had Queen when you were a teenager, after all, and Led Zeppelin. And Whitesnake . . . no, that was the eighties."

"How did you know I'm a Zeppelin fan? And we will not discuss the so-called music of David Coverdale on my watch. And why have we gone off on this odd tangent?" he added. Then he pulled her close and kissed her, because he couldn't take it anymore.

Sweet goddess, she was delicious!

And he was greedy for the taste of her. It wasn't just a kiss he needed; the pulsing rush of blood beneath soft skin called to him.

He moved with her until they were hid-den behind one of the wide concrete pillars, and all the time he kept his mouth pressed against hers, drinking in the sweet heat of her. She clung just as greedily to him, and arched against him when his hand came up beneath her blouse to caress her breasts. Her nipples were already stiff and he teased them to harder points, drawing a long moan from her. He drew even more excitement from arousing her. Her thigh ground against his erection, and it was his turn to groan.

Phillipa was overwhelmed by the swift intensity of her arousal; an orgasm shot through her at the speed of light. It left her shaking, only half in possession of her senses. She pulled her head back from Matt's and pressed her hands against his chest.

"Whoa! Slow down! I'm embarrassing me!"

"Why?" he demanded, his voice a tight growl. "We need each other."

She gave a swift look around the garage. No one was in sight, but they could be interrupted at any moment. She had a crazy vision of slipping to her knees and giving the man a blow job right here — the man drove her to distraction, tempting her to do things she'd never dared before. But she was stronger than temptation, right?

"I'm happy to perform any lewd and lascivious acts you have in mind," she told him. "But not here."

He backed up a step and took a few deep

breaths. "Right," he said. "You're right. It's just that I've been out of my mind ever since you fainted yesterday and —"

"You *were* here!"

"Yes, I —"

"I didn't dream that?"

Oh, goddess, Matt thought. *Marc and I were in full hunting mode. How much did she see?*

He stepped toward her, ready to give her a glib explanation or wipe the whole incident from her mind if necessary. When her eyes widened at his approach, he thought for a nanosecond that it was with fear. Then he realized that she was looking past him.

He moved at the same moment she shouted, "Down!"

He heard the bullet whiz past his shoulder and felt the heat of its passage. He grabbed Phillipa around the waist, and they darted around the pillar together. The first bullet plowed into a car door. The second hit the pillar, sending up a spray of concrete dust.

"Silencer," Phillipa complained.

"Which impedes the accuracy of an inexperienced shooter," Matt pointed out.

She opened her mouth to reply, closed it forcefully, then said, "Not a good time for a technical discussion."

"Agreed."

Matt held Phillipa firmly against the pillar as he peered cautiously around it. He wasn't afraid of the attacker or the weapon for his own sake, but he was terrified for Phillipa's sake. He was *not* going to let anything happen to her. It was time to end this thing.

"Don't move," he ordered.

But as he stepped away from the pillar, the elevator door slid open, three people walked out into the garage, and the metal gate to the street started to lift. The shooter broke and ran for the gate, the car that entered giving him cover.

Matt snarled and grabbed Phillipa by the hand. By the time they got outside, the attacker was already inside a large white van with the engine running.

Matt could have reached him, but he was not going to leave Phillipa alone for a second. Purists roamed in packs.

The van was moving by the time he pulled Phillipa to his car and pushed her inside. The van had turned onto the street when his own car reached the lot exit. As he turned to follow, he had to stomp hard on the brakes to avoid hitting a car entering the lot.

"Bloody sodding hell!" he shouted.

The woman driving the other car lay on the horn and gave him a blistering look, all the while blocking the turn he needed to make.

He revved the engine and made a rude gesture, and woman finally took the hint and pulled all the way into the parking lot.

By the time he pulled out into traffic, the damn van was nowhere in sight.

Michele tried not to laugh at the furious driver she'd just blocked, though his reaction was very satisfying. Since he had the Elliot woman with him, he was clearly the enemy. He was probably one of the vampires that had foiled their original plan, but she wasn't sure about that yet. Elliot was known to have friends in the Las Vegas police force. Whoever her protector was, if he had to die for Andrew's mission to be completed, so be it.

It was a good thing she had decided to act as backup when Andrew went on the hunt. The mission had been given to him; she knew in her soul that he was the one who had to carry it out. Britney was also right about hunters needing to work together, though. It was how they had survived against the overwhelming strength of the vampires for centuries.

But Britney was too much of a hothead; she'd taken a personal grudge against Phillipa Elliot from the first. Michele couldn't be sure that Britney wouldn't get in Andrew's way.

"So I'll have your back as long as you need me, my boy," she murmured. Even though she was tired and wanted to go home to San Diego.

Duty first.

And for now, duty meant turning her car around and following Elliot and the man who was searching for Andrew.

CHAPTER
TWENTY-FIVE

Mike had never woken up to find a wolf staring him in the eye before. Not a were-wolf, but a *wolf.* He'd never actually met a real wolf before, but he recognized the scent even before he opened his eyes and saw the animal.

Then he remembered what he was, and began to wonder where he was. And he saw the bars of the cage.

Shit!

He was up and snarling in a moment. The wolf was on the outside, he was on the inside, and the cage reeked of cat. It was a big cage, since it held him standing upright, so it must be a big cat.

There was a growl from the other side of the cage, and he turned his head to look.

There were *two* wolves waiting outside the cage. They were guarding him, weren't they? As if they'd have a chance, if he were to get out. But the cage was so sturdy and strong, there wasn't a chance of his getting out. So the wolves were perfectly safe.

He was safe from them, too, he supposed, even though the pair glared at him with domineering menace. He ignored them, and forgot about them altogether when he spotted the large metal dishes in the cage. He was drawn to the water like a magnet and gulped down every drop of it, before he turned to the bowl of meat and finished it off just as quickly. He was so thirsty and famished that the idea of drugs or poison didn't occur to him until the meal was already done.

Too late now, I guess.

He yawned, replete, and realized that while his flank ached, the pain wasn't so bad anymore. The fur had been shaved from the wounded area, and the wound itself had been cleaned. It smelled of disinfectant, and a topical cream had been smeared on it as well.

His captor could have killed him; instead he'd taken care of him.

Beyond the cage, beyond the watching wolves, he saw that he was a prisoner in what looked like a luxurious studio apartment. For some reason, there were a lot of flowers and stuffed animals in the place. What was that all about?

And the vampire was a Cage, some distant relative of Matt Bridger's. Mike recognized a trace of the Family pheromone permeating the room. But the Cages were a large family, and Mike had no reason to trust the vampire just because he was kin to his partner. Especially since this particular vampire had captured him and locked him up.

He needed to figure out a way to escape. Out of the cage somehow, then out the door. He badly missed having thumbs. Somehow he doubted he was going to be able to gnaw through steel bars meant to hold lions or tigers or some such revolting feline creature.

What was he supposed to do — laze around letting the vampire feed him and tend his wound, and wait for his chance? He didn't have the patience for that — but he might not have any other choice.

Luckily, he soon sensed the approach of the Cage vampire. The wolves did as well, and they were waiting by the door, tails wagging excitedly, when the vampire entered.

The first thing Cage did was drop to his knees and pet the wolves. "Did you miss me?" he asked as they wriggled like puppies under his hands and licked his face. "Did you keep our guest company? You didn't try to play dominance games with a werewolf, did you? Of course you didn't."

Cage and the canines' enthusiasm for each other was disgusting. It annoyed Mike that the vampire greeted the animals before paying attention to him, and he growled to show his displeasure.

That got Cage's attention, but it also made him laugh. "Did you wake up on the wrong side of the bed?" he asked as he got to his feet and approached the cage.

I didn't get a bed. Mike bumped his head against the cage door.

But Cage didn't take this obvious hint to let him out. Instead, he crouched down until he was at eye level with Mike. "That's odd," he said. "I assumed you'd morph back to human eventually, after I knocked you out."

Mike bared his fangs, showing his displeasure at having been rendered unconscious.

The vampire sat down cross-legged in front of the cage. "I'm Jason Cage." He held out a hand. "And you are?"

What did this guy want, for him to shake paws? The vampire reached to touch his head, and Mike backed quickly away from any contact telepathy. Oh, no — no vampire was getting into his head, even if he had to

241

gnaw the bastard's hands off to keep from being touched.

"We really need to talk," Cage went on. "It'd be simpler for both of us if you'd morph back to human." He gave a thin smile. "I'm sure I have something you could wear. And I might even let you out of the tiger pen."

Mike was anything but amused. Why had the vampire locked him up in the first place? And where had he heard the name Jason Cage before?

From Matt, he thought, and Matthias Bridger didn't tend to deal with the nicer members of the vampire population. Great — so there was more than one bad-guy vampire in town. Wait a minute, how many vampires had been at the bank robbery? His wolf memory wasn't the most reliable thing in the world.

"It's very inconvenient that I wasn't able to capture your friend as well. I don't particularly want to deal with two of your kind at once, but one or both of you is responsible for murder, and that has to be dealt with."

This guy didn't make any sense. If he'd been at the bank robbery, he already knew about the human-slaying werewolf. They worked together, didn't they?

"Not that seeing you punished is exactly my problem. For that we'll have to call in the tracker."

I am *the tracker, you idiot!*

"But I guess I have to take responsibility for catching —"

A phone rang, interrupting this soliloquy. The vampire gave an annoyed look toward the table where the phone sat, but by the third ring he reluctantly got up to answer it.

"I really don't need to be disturbed right now, Sonja." After listening for a moment, he said, "You're right, that is important. I'll be right there."

No, Mike thought. You can't leave now! Talk to me!

Jason Cage turned back toward Mike after hanging up the phone. "I've got to see about a tiger with a bad tummy ache." He patted his pet wolves on their heads. "Howl if your cousin here makes any trouble, okay?"

But it was Mike who howled as Jason Cage left the room, in utter, complete frustration.

CHAPTER
TWENTY-SIX

"I missed you," Phillipa said.

Damn! That was a stupid thing to say. Especially since she'd seen him just twenty-four hours ago, at the airport. Where he'd been anxious to catch an outbound flight.

"What are you still doing in town, anyway?" she demanded.

"I missed you, too," he replied.

His gaze was firmly on the road, and his hands were tightly gripping the steering wheel. He was tense and angry, and it radiated from him like heat; she was feeling much the same. They had lost the white van before they even managed to turn onto the street, but Bridger was still trying to pick up a trail. She didn't try to talk him out of it.

Her own thoughts were zinging around a hundred subjects at once. She was trying desperately to pull up details from her memory. She had a thousand questions. She needed answers, but everything kept coming back to — Matthias Bridger.

"Why didn't you leave?" she asked him.

She hated that her tone sounded more than a little petulant. She didn't want him gone, yet her emotions were less complicated when he wasn't around. Okay, maybe her emotions were just as complicated, and centered around an aching need to be with him — but she could at least think in a reasonable fashion. Being with him sent her hormones into overdrive and kept her thought processes too screwed up for reasonable use.

"I meant to leave."

Matt hated that his tone sounded more than a little apologetic. It wasn't his fault he and Phillipa were together right now. Being together meant fighting the attraction. Being apart meant having to fight the attraction as well, but distance ought to ease some of the pain. At least, that had been the plan.

"I think I'm an idiot," he muttered. "A stubborn, ridiculous fool. But enough about me — what were you doing in that garage?"

"Looking for evidence," she answered.

"That isn't your job. You aren't with the Las Vegas police force."

Her glare was scorching. "What were *you* doing there?"

He had the feeling she wasn't just talking about today. "Looking for evidence. And it *is* my job, even if I am not with the Las Vegas police force. But the evidence found us."

"And now we've lost him."

Matt didn't agree with the plural, but he agreed that giving up the search made sense. He gestured toward the GPS screen in the center of the dash. "Do you know how to make that thing work?"

Phillipa studied it for a moment. "Yes."

"Good." He gave her an address, and she pushed buttons. Soon a map appeared on the screen, and voice directions issued from a speaker.

"I dislike having an auto talk to me," Matt complained, but he drove as the bland female voice instructed.

Phillipa couldn't help but smile. Here was something else she and the Brit agreed on. "Technology has gotten a bit uppity, hasn't it?"

"Most definitely."

She sat back and closed her eyes against the brutal sunlight that made her head ache. She was tempted to ask if she could borrow Bridger's sunglasses, but she supposed the driver needed them more than she did. The adrenaline rush was fading, leaving her tired, and thirsty.

"Where are we heading?" she asked, glancing his way.

His jaw set stubbornly before he answered. "I'm taking you to a safe house."

She tilted her head curiously. "And what do I need a safe house for?"

"You were the one being shot at."

She considered arguing, but it was hard to do so when she *had* been shot at, for the second time in as many days. So she leaned her head back against the leather seat and closed her eyes once more. It helped her to think when she wasn't looking at Bridger.

Why isn't she fighting me on this? Matt wondered. The fact that she wasn't being adamant and making demands was deeply disturbing. Modern mortal women did not simply acquiesce to being taken care of, no matter how well that suited their vampire lovers' primal instincts.

The old-fashioned part of him was relieved that she put herself in his hands — but he also knew that the old-fashioned part of himself was a fool to be lulled into thinking he was completely in control of the situation. He wouldn't be in control until he knew exactly what she was up to.

He was very tempted to goad her into an argument for the sake of exploring her mind. But she looked tired, and he hated disturbing her just because he was uneasy. Sentimental, romantic foolishness, of course . . . but he spent the drive out of the city stealing glances at Phillipa, drinking in the sheer pleasure of her presence.

Eventually the GPS told him to make one last turn onto a long dirt drive, and he stopped the car in front of a low house surrounded by scrub trees and cacti, hidden from the highway by a low hill.

"We're here," he announced.

Phillipa opened the door before he could do it for her, but he did reach her side as she got out of the car. She gave him an odd look as he took her by the arm, but she didn't comment on how quickly he'd moved. She let him lead her into the house, but once they were inside, she shook off his touch. She crossed the wooden floor until she was well away from him, standing next to a window, and turned her back on him.

He didn't realize that she had a mobile telephone clipped to her belt until she'd already flipped it open and pushed a speed dial button.

"If you're calling the police —" he began.

She continued to ignore him. "Jo, hi, it's me."

Matt sighed with relief. Until —

248

"Josephine, is Marcus a vampire?"

Matt was too stunned to snatch the telephone from her. He could only stand there during the tense silence that followed, and then listen to Josephine Cage's reply to her older sister.

A quiet but firm, "Yes."

"Thank you." Phillipa put the phone away and slowly turned to face Matt. Though her expression was still completely neutral, anger seethed close to the surface. "*Now* we can have that argument you've been waiting for."

Chapter
Twenty-Seven

"It's not what you think," he said.

"You don't know *what* I think. Though I suppose you could find out if you want to," Phillipa added. "You being a vampire, and telepathic, and — stuff."

Matt came forward and held out his hand. She frowned, but gave up her mobile phone. He pocketed it. "Obscuring thoughts and memories is permitted for our kind to preserve the secret of our existence," he informed her. "But invading a person's mind is a punishable offense. So yes, I could find out your thoughts, but no, I won't. What I think you think is that vampires can't be the evil monsters of legend, or you wouldn't be alone in the middle of nowhere in the power of one of them. You are not a stupid woman, Phillipa Elliot."

She reached into her pocket. He wondered if she was going to bring out a cross or garlic, but she took out a piece of hard candy, unwrapped it, and popped it in her mouth. "I need some carbs," she said after sucking on the sweet for a bit. "I've been thinking about Brandon," she said after she swallowed. "Actually, I've been wondering how I could tell my parents that their eldest grandchild is the spawn of Satan. Then I remembered what my brothers were like as kids, and it occurred to me that they might not even notice."

She moved across the room and took a seat in a deeply upholstered living room chair. He followed and sat down facing her on the nearby couch. He could feel a great deal of turmoil beneath her calm exterior.

"I'm wondering when the hysteria is going to erupt," he told her.

She folded her hands in her lap, and lifted her chin. "I am trying to remain calm. Stress makes my blood glucose shoot up like a rocket."

"Then what about the argument you promised me?" he teased. "I always look forward to a bit of fireworks. They make lovely foreplay." Before she could respond to this, he added, "Our goddesschild is not the spawn of the devil, though I imagine he will be an unbearably spoiled brat."

Her folded hands clenched until the knuckles went white. "My nephew really is a vampire?"

"No."

"I mean, how is that possible?" She didn't seem to have heard him. "How could vampires reproduce?" She shot to her feet. "Oh, my God, my sister's been sleeping with a vampire!"

"So have you," he pointed out. He got up and put his hands on her shoulders. He meant to gently push her back into her chair, but the need to keep on touching her was too strong. So he faced her with his hands on her, and gave in to his own curiosity. "When did you first suspect? How did you figure it out?"

She moved closer to him, though he doubted she knew she did so. "When did I suspect?" Her expression went out of focus as she thought back. "At Jo and Marc's wedding. I knew something was wrong, even then. Everyone was too perfect, too beautiful, too young, too masculine, too feminine, too — everything."

"You shouldn't have noticed," he said. "At least, you shouldn't be able to remember us that way. We had some very good professional telepaths working that party."

"I know when something is true," she said. "It all seemed perfectly reasonable at the time, but the weirdness stayed in the back

252

of my head. Then there was the sex with you."

He smiled. "You were overwhelmed by my prowess."

She snorted, but admitted, "Yes, I was, actually. It was — is — like nothing else I've ever experienced. Can sex be too good?"

"Not when you find the right partner," he told her.

He burned to make love to her right now, to show her how right they were together. He settled for giving her a swift, hard kiss. "What other clues did you follow, Officer Elliot?"

She took a deep, steadying breath. He was aware of her racing pulse. "You call me sweet," she said. "Is that because you've tasted my blood?"

"That's one of the reasons I think you're sweet." He touched the tip of her pert, upturned nose. "Is my sweet tooth one of your clues?"

"It wasn't, until just now. But there were so many other things. One of them was Marc telling me that I needed a vampire boyfriend. I thought he was joking."

"He was matchmaking. Just because he's happily bonded to a mortal —"

Phillipa frowned. "What's *bonded?* Has

he forced Jo into anything?"

"What do you mean by anything?"

She blushed and looked away. Then she cleared her throat and looked him in the eye. "Is my sister a vampire's sex slave?"

Matt threw back his head and laughed. "Does she act like a sex slave?"

"I don't know what they do in the privacy of their bedroom. And I don't really want to know," she told him, "unless he forced her into this bonding thing."

"It can't be forced," he said, and sighed. "A bond is true love, and cannot be denied."

"Oh, crap. I suspected it was something like that. So if I put a stake through Marc's heart, Jo would be really pissed at me."

"To kill him would be the same as killing her. What other clues?" he asked, wanting to distract Phillipa from the subject of vampire love.

"The baptism ceremony. It certainly wasn't like any rite from any religion I know about. And then there was the guy who came up to me at the airport and told me that my sister was damned because of the vampire. Among his exact words were, 'They want all our beautiful women to be their sex slaves.' "

"Not all of the women," Matt said. "And we only take volunteers. I also don't see

254

where damnation has anything to do with it. I'm sure you assumed that this man was completely mad."

"Until I discovered he was telling the truth about vampires. Of course, by then he'd started shooting at my sister and nephew. Oh, and I thought I was dreaming when I saw you vamp-out in the garage, but that wasn't a dream. Not yesterday, or today, when I saw you move too fast to be human when the guy was shooting at us again."

"Ah, you noticed."

"And you were wearing sunglasses in a place where the lighting wasn't all that bright. That's very cool in a *Matrix* sort of way, but it's not normal human behavior."

"Would you kindly stop using the word *human* as if you and I are from different species?"

"We are, aren't we?"

"Would we be interested in mating if we were? Would Marcus and Josephine have a child if we were?" He pulled her close and pressed his hips against her. "I'm not dead yet."

"Yeah, I can feel that."

He gave a low, wicked chuckle and whirled her toward the couch. "Maybe I should prove it, instead."

Phillipa smiled, and her arms came

around him as they landed on the soft cushions. "Yeah. Maybe you should."

CHAPTER
TWENTY-EIGHT

It was very hard to pace inside a cage, but Mike had to do *some*thing or go crazy. Where the hell was that damned vampire?

The wolves, aware of his dangerous mood, had disappeared behind a counter. Every now and then one of them would stick its head around a corner to check him out. Mike would growl, and the wolf would duck back. It wasn't much entertainment, but it was something to do.

While he paced and wished for Cage's return, he racked his brain trying to recall what he knew about this Family vampire. Jason was his name — but Matt had called him something else, hadn't he? Sandor, or Sandor's son . . . Sanderson . . . yeah, that was the term Matt used. Along with "stupid," "idiot," and "kid." What was it he had done?

He remembered just as Cage came back into the room, and would have laughed if he could.

"Why are you still in wolf morph?" Cage asked as he came over to sit by the cage again. He looked as impatient as Mike felt. "Do you think that shape offers an excuse for what you've done? From what I've heard about werewolf justice, that isn't going to help your case any."

No it wouldn't — if *I* was the one responsible for the killings.

Cage got up and went to his wolves.

Mike was furious at being ignored while the vampire fussed with the furballs, and he began to howl. The wolves soon joined in. What he expressed in werespeak was anger and frustration. The wolves' howls were a mixture of anxiety and sympathy. *They* understood the problem. Why didn't the freakin' vampire?

Fortunately, the vampire seemed to understand his wolves. After he managed to get them calmed down, he came back to Mike.

"You're stuck in wolf morph, aren't you? You can't change."

Mike nodded.

"How is that possible? Brain damage?"

Mike let out a small snarl, then remembered that he needed this guy. *Go get help, Lassie!* he thought at the vampire.

But Cage preferred touch telepathy, didn't

258

he? Mike did not, not with another species, and especially not after having been mind-raped. But there was no escaping the contact if he wanted to get into his human shape again. He gritted his teeth and moved to the front of the cage, then pressed his head against the bars, hoping the vampire would take the hint.

He did.

Mike closed his eyes when Cage reached out to touch his head. The expected intrusion didn't come. He didn't feel a thing, other than the pleasant warmth and pressure of the contact. What was the matter? Had this guy lost all the psychic talent Matt had told him about?

Cage's hand jerked back as if he'd been bit. "You know Bridger?"

Mike stared Cage in the eye, and the vampire put his hand back on Mike's head.

After a few more minutes of Mike feeling absolutely nothing, the vampire shot to his feet. This time he was the one who paced like a trapped animal. His wolves had ventured from behind the counter, but they got out of Cage's way and disappeared again.

Cage's agitation got on Mike's nerves as well. He growled to get the vampire's attention.

Cage turned to confront him. "I cannot help you."

Mike could tell from the way Jason Cage spoke, from the way he radiated tension, that he *could* help. Mike lowered his head menacingly and stared at the vampire, fangs bared in a silent snarl.

"I can't!" Cage paced some more before turning back to him. "Do you know how much trouble I got into the last time I messed with somebody's head?"

Mike nodded.

"Bridger told you?"

Mike nodded again. He hoped his association with the Prime who had put Cage away hadn't earned him an enemy. Help me, he thought, and pawed at the cage door.

Cage studied him and rubbed his jaw thoughtfully. Then he moved forward and opened the animal pen.

The temptation was strong to make a dash toward the door, but escape didn't really lie that way. Mike held down his sense of panic and urgency and stepped carefully, slowly, out of the cage. He walked up to Cage and butted him in the knee with his head. The vampire's hand automatically came down to pet him, and Mike let him do it. He aimed his thoughts squarely at Cage at the contact.

Help me! You can do it.

"It's forbidden to go that deeply into another mind."

How do you think this happened? A vampire did this to me. A vampire can fix it.

"Let Bridger do it." Cage gave a bitter laugh.

Help me, Mike insisted.

Cage moved across the room. Mike growled, and followed.

When they reached a couch, Cage gestured. "Have a seat."

The cushions smelled of wolf. How nice to know that pets were allowed on the furniture. Mike's sore flank twinged when he jumped, but he got up on the couch and lay down.

Cage took a seat on the floor next to him, then put his hands on Mike's head. "If this works, I'll probably be in deep trouble." He sighed. "And if it doesn't work, I can always use you in my act. Close your eyes," he went on soothingly. "Go to sleep."

Mike didn't want to go to sleep, but he did. Once asleep, he had a long, dark, and terrible dream. There was screaming. Something awful chased him across a barren landscape while a storm raged all around. A lightning bolt crackled out of the sky. He tried to dodge, but the force pursuing him drove him forward, and the lightning lanced through him. He had to be dying, it hurt so bad, and the universe went dark.

When he woke up, Mike had a terrible headache. He sat up and pressed his hands against his aching temples.

"What the hell have I been drinking?"

"Would you like some coffee?" Cage asked.

He caught the heavenly scent of it and looked up. "Good God, yes."

Hands.

He held them out in front of him. He had hands!

"I'm back."

"You are," Cage said, and held out a full mug.

Mike grinned at the vampire and took the coffee. It felt marvelous to have thumbs! "Damn, kid, you're a good wizard."

"Kid?" Cage's head lifted proudly with typical Prime arrogance. "Kid?"

Mike remembered that Cage was a good forty to fifty years his senior. "Sorry. Matt thinks of you as a kid."

Cage looked annoyed, then he grinned. "Yeah, well, Bridger's an old geezer. Where do you know my cousin from? How do you know about me?"

Mike took a sip of coffee while Cage took

a seat on a nearby chair. "I know that Matt spent most of World War II chasing you all over Europe after you pulled that hypnotizing-the-Nazi stunt."

"It was a stupid stunt," Cage admitted. "I was young, and trying to save the world. If I'd been a Clan Prime, I might have gotten away with using my power for good. Tony Crowe fought in the war, and he didn't get in trouble for it."

"Tony Crowe didn't hypnotize Rudolf Hess into taking a plane and defecting to England."

Cage shrugged. "It seemed like a good idea at the time. The Romany my family had lived among for generations were being murdered. I had to do something."

"You used your gifts to interfere with mortal history."

"I used my gifts to convince a crazy occultist Nazi to seek a peace agreement. It might have worked too, if Churchill hadn't turned out to have vampire blood on his mother's side, and figured out what was going on. He's the one who set Bridger on me. Do you know Tony?" he added.

Mike nodded. "I work with his daughter, Sid Wolf. That is, I work with her when I get a chance to do my day job. I'm Mike Bleythin," he added.

Cage looked uncomfortable for a moment. "I found that out while I was inside your head." He gave a respectful nod. "Welcome to Las Vegas, Tracker."

Mike couldn't help but smile at the vampire's apologetic attitude. "If you'd managed to catch that other werewolf, too, my job here would be done."

"So you are in town to solve that problem."

Mike nodded.

"But what does a werewolf have to do with the bank robbers?"

Mike just smiled. He was grateful for Cage's help, but that didn't give the vampire a need to know werewolf business. Except that there were other vampires involved, Mike recalled.

"What do you know about the werewolf problem?" he asked.

Cage's wolves had come out of hiding and were seated on either side of his chair, where he rubbed his fingers through their fur. "When a wolf was spotted at a bank robbery, the police consulted me as a wolf expert."

"Why would they do that?"

Cage patted the wolves' on the head. "I do a stage show that features George and Gracie here."

"And lions and tigers and bears?" Mike asked with a sniff.

"No bears."

Mike glanced around. "This is your dressing room?" Cage nodded. "What's with all the stuffed animals?"

Cage gave the piles of plush tigers and lions a wave. "Gifts from teenage girl fans," he explained. "When I can't take the clutter anymore, I donate whatever George and Gracie don't shred to a local hospital."

Vampires could be such softies. Which was a good thing for the world, when you considered what the bad ones could do with their gifts. The question was, was this vampire enough of a good guy for Mike to trust him with information about who the bank robbers really were? He owed the guy, and if Matt wasn't in town, then Cage's help could come in handy.

But Mike didn't know the personal dynamics of the local vampire population. Even if Cage wasn't involved in the crimes, it was a sure bet he was involved one way or another with the ones who were. Vampires didn't have the pack mentality of werefolk, but loyalty to your own kind was a necessary mind-set when you were among the smallest and most despised minorities in the world.

"Did you know Matt Bridger was in town? And if he's left yet?"

Cage didn't look pleased at the mention of Bridger. "He's here, and he's gone all official on us while he neutralizes some Purists that broke the truce."

Well, wasn't that interesting? It seemed that Matt wasn't aware of the bad vampires in the neighborhood but was after mortals instead. This didn't smell right.

"Then can I use your phone?" Mike stood up and noticed that he was naked. "And borrow some clothes?" He checked his thigh and saw a livid scar, but the wound itself was healed. Good. He was back to normal in every way.

"In a minute." Cage rose to his feet, and the wolves headed back behind the counter. "First, you better make sure you really are free of the spell."

Mike hated the stab of fear that went through him at the thought of doing something that should be as easy as breathing. He recognized the fear as residue of the trap. He was free, but still scared to morph! Damn, that bitch had done a number on him.

Right before she'd put a spell on him, he'd been thinking that staying in wolf form forever was appealing. Being trapped in his animal body had cured him of *that* temptation.

"I don't want to be a wolf," he said.

Cage gestured toward his lurking canines. "They're wolves, you're not. Change."

The damned vampire was right. He had to know he could do it, and trying it here would be safe. He was safe here, right? He had to trust that. And believe he could morph at will. No, he had to *know* he could.

He swore. Then he took a deep breath and let his body flow from one form into another.

It wasn't hard at all. And frankly, the room smelled better to his human nose.

So he took another deep breath, and changed back. "Satisfied?" he asked the watching vampire.

"Completely," Cage answered. "Although you would have made a great addition to my act."

CHAPTER
TWENTY-NINE

"We need to talk."

"Now?" Matt asked, and took Phillipa's nipple into his mouth.

"Okay, later," she agreed, breathless and burning.

Somewhere along the line they had rolled off the couch and onto the floor, and managed to pull off all their clothes.

Phillipa ran her hands through his hair, and across the magnificent width of his shoulders. She'd never known anything to feel as wonderful as touching him. Except that being touched by him was maybe, just maybe, a little bit more wonderful.

"I'm making love to a vampire."

I'm making love to a vampire! Wait until I tell Jo.

Wait until I get my hands on Jo. What was she thinking? Why didn't she tell me?

Matt's head lifted from her breast, and she saw the glitter of amusement in his narrow green eyes.

Then he kissed her, and all she could think about for a while was how much she never wanted him to stop kissing her.

"You've bitten me, haven't you?" she asked when his mouth left hers.

"I have, I confess," he answered. "Several times." He kissed a line from her temple down to the base of her throat.

"I thought so." She laughed. "Now I know why Jo wanted to know if we'd done anything kinky."

"Kinky?" His eyes glittered laughter at her again. "Woman, *not* tasting you would be kinky."

"Tasting." She repeated the word. "I like how that sounds. Sexy, instead of — kinky."

"If you want to get kinky, love, I'm sure we can come up with something to satisfy your tastes."

"I'm sure we can. Later," she told him, with a wicked smile. "Let me get used to this 'my boyfriend is a vampire' thing before I show you my fur-lined handcuffs."

"Boyfriend!" He sounded affronted. "I think I'm a bit more than that."

A thrill went through her as this declaration, but she managed to keep her tone light as she asked, "Is that a proposal?"

He laughed. "I don't need to propose."

"Why, you arrogant —"

He bit her shoulder, and the explosion of pleasure cut off anything she might have to say.

Okay, she didn't need a proposal, she thought, when she came back down to earth. What she wanted was *this,* all the time.

"God, I missed you," she whispered against his chest.

"I thought it was best to walk away — fool that I am."

His hands moved over her, his mouth slowly teased down her body, and the heat of need began to build again. She whimpered when he shifted away from her.

"I should have done this a long time ago," he said.

Her puzzlement was answered when his wrist pressed against her mouth. There was suddenly blood on her lips, and the heat and scent tempted her tongue. The taste of him was hot and sweet at once, and full of fire.

She was an Arizona girl, she adored everything hot and spicy. She clamped her mouth around his wrist, and suckled hard.

It was better than twelve-year-old scotch or hundred-year-old brandy. Better than champagne, or double-shot espresso, or any drug she could imagine.

He tasted of honey and tequila, mixed with lava shot through with radioactive isotopes.

And this vintage was made just for her.

She drank in Matthias — his life, his soul, his dreams and his hopes, his fears and frustrations, and most of all, his deep need to be completely one with her.

When he took his wrist away, she began to cry.

He grasped her tightly to him. "I know," he whispered. "I know." He let out a deep, heart-wrenching sigh. "We'll never be alone again."

The intensity of his tone brought her head up, and she looked into his eyes.

She brushed damp hair from his forehead, and his eyes closed on a shudder. "Matt, you're terrified."

He kissed her temple, then her nose. "My dear, you have no idea."

Then his lips claimed hers again, and she forgot thoughts and words.

Their bodies shifted, and her hips rose to meet his hard, piercing thrust. As he moved inside her, she rode the rising spiral of sensation that took her to another place where all that they were met, joined, and explosively shattered.

CHAPTER THIRTY

"You're right, Matthias, I have no idea."

Phillipa's voice drifted to him from a long way off. He loved the sound of her voice. And the soft pillow of her breast against his cheek, and the scent of her skin. When her words finally sank in, he realized he was going to have to come back from this pleasant, drifting place and face some real-world problems. He didn't want to.

"More sex," he mumbled, "less talk."

"How old are you?" she asked.

"Um — one hundred thirty-something." Maybe closer to one hundred and fifty; he couldn't quite remember. He began to caress her for their mutual pleasure, and to distract her if possible.

"Which means you're somewhat beyond adolescence in vampire years, am I right?" There was a catch in her voice, but he could tell she wasn't going to be distracted.

"I'm a bit long in the fang, as a friend

recently put it."

She laughed, and ran her hands down his back. There was more comfort in her touch than anything he had ever known. "I've been looking for you for a long time," she told him. "When I lived in London, I used to wander around with this sense of anticipation. I thought it was just because I loved the city so much — but now I realize that the exciting *something* I was waiting to find around every corner was really you. How is that possible?" She laughed again. "Or am I just being a total romantic twit?"

"Never a *total* twit." He lifted his head to look at her. "Besides, if I'd seen you coming, I would have run for cover."

She frowned at him. "Why? What are you afraid of? Girl humans and boy vampires obviously work." She laughed, but nervousness underlaid the humor. "Marc was matchmaking, but Jo tried to warn me off." She tilted her head. "Which has something to do with why you don't want this, this — thing — we have."

"This *thing* is called bonding."

"Which means . . . we were born to be together? Body, mind, and soul?"

He nodded as he touched the tip of her pert nose. "Perceptive wench, aren't you?"

"I've watched Marc and Jo together. They

seem so different, yet I can't imagine them being with anyone else. There's a connection between them, like we have. Why doesn't Jo want us to be together?"

"For your sake," he answered. "I have a reputation among our kind."

"As a womanizer? A drunk? Gambler? What? It's explanation time, Matthias." She shoved against his shoulders. "Move over; you're heavy. It's not like you're some dinky little elf boy. *Are* there elves?" she added as he rolled off of her, then helped her to her feet. Their fingers stayed twined together after they were standing.

Matt shrugged. "If there are, they certainly wouldn't travel in the same social circles as vampires."

He went to put his hands on her waist, but she backed away and began to gather her scattered clothing. Accepting that she needed some armor to face their situation, he got dressed as well.

When he was done, he glanced out the window and saw that day had turned into night. Making love to this woman was too distracting. Dangerously distracting, although being with her was the most wonderful thing that had ever happened to him.

"I have a job to do," he told her. "Explanations are going to have to wait."

274

"Bullshit."

He raised an eyebrow in surprise. "I beg your pardon?"

She ticked points off on her fingers as she answered. "Jo is safe. The baby is safe. I am safely with you, in a safe house. Yes, the bad guys are still out there, but nobody is in danger from them at the moment. So talk to me." She flipped on a lamp, then sat on the couch and folded her hands in her lap.

She looked so earnest he almost laughed, and so determined, he knew he didn't dare do anything else if he wanted to get back on the job anytime soon.

"Let's see, where do I start?" he asked. "You now know that vampires are real, and that Bram Stoker got most of the details wrong. We are long-lived but not immortal. We are born, not made, and can't turn anyone else into vampires. Science keeps us from being burned by sunlight. The people hunting you are called Purists. They're a splinter group among the mortal vampire hunters, but mortals don't generally hunt vampires anymore. Some vampires *do* need hunting, which is my job." He smiled. "When vampires break our laws, I'm the cop that gets called in. Since the Purists have now broken the long-standing truce between vampires and mortals, it's also my job to bring them to justice. Besides, as Brandon's guardian, it is my duty to protect him."

"And mine," Phillipa pointed out. "I'm also Brandon's guardian."

Matt's first impulse was to argue with her, but he couldn't. *Damn it by all the demons of day, the woman was right!*

"So you are," Matt acknowledged with a stiff nod. "But —"

She pointed a warning finger at him.

He raised his hands in submission. "Fine. We'll get the bastards together."

At least if he kept her by his side, it would be easier to protect her. It was very, very frustrating to know that he had no right to keep her completely out of harm's way. By the Mother of the Moon, why had the Matri and Elders decided it was all right to allow mortal guardians for half-mortal children?

"Because the kids are equal parts mortal and vampire?" Phillipa guessed.

Matt was startled at her picking up his thought. But she was bound to pick up on his stronger thoughts and emotions as their bond grew deeper, wasn't she? Now that they had shared blood —

"What does your as-yet-unexplained reputation have to do with being bonded?"

Goddess, but she was persistent!

"It's known that I've never wanted a bondmate. Your sister was trying to protect you from my well-earned love-them-and-leave-them rep. But since we first had sex, I've learned the hard way that there's no fighting the need to bond. I never intended to stay with you. But once bitten, the taste for you was too strong."

"I see."

"Not that I haven't tried to keep away from you."

She looked stricken, and asked in a tight voice, "Why? Would you prefer one of your own? Octavia, perhaps?"

Her fear of rejection hit him like a blow. "No! I didn't mean it like that."

Though he wasn't quite sure what *that* was. Even with telepathy and the other psychic gifts of his kind, dealing with women was confusing. Especially dealing with this woman, because with Phillipa he had to get it right. Maybe they were bonding, but that didn't make them of one mind.

"I don't want to see you hurt," he told her. "I don't want to get you killed." He began to pace as a gruesome memory came back to him, one he was unfortunately going to have to share. He came to stand in front of her. "In my job, there's only one cop at a time. There's a very low crime rate

277

among vampires."

He was tempted to veer off the subject and explain that he was only talking about the Families. But this wasn't the time to get into the history and practices of the three different vampire cultures.

"But those who *do* commit crimes tend to be dangerous, vicious, arrogant, egotistical, vengeful bastards. They don't take kindly to being brought down. They take it very personally. And they always vow to get even. Some can be rehabilitated, but some . . ." He shook his head.

"I know the type," she told him. "I've put a few people away who vowed to get me when they get out." She gave an offhand shrug. "Threats are part of the job."

"And accepting the danger for myself is part of *my* job," he told her. "But I *will not* put anyone else in harm's way."

She gave him a deep, assessing look. "What happened to get you so spooked?"

"When I was an apprentice, the Prime who was training me fell in love with a mortal woman and began bonding with her. One of his enemies took revenge by murdering the Prime's lover. He slit her throat."

He could still see the dark red stain spread across the carpet, smell the stench of lifeless blood, but he couldn't put the full horror of the crime into words.

Yet his perceptive Phillipa understood. "Blood is sacred," she said. "Instead of taking her blood, the bastard showed his contempt by letting her bleed out."

Matt nodded. "I killed the bastard when I caught him, but the woman was dead, and the Prime who loved her was broken. I vowed I would never love anyone. Because I wasn't going to be the cause of an innocent woman's death."

She was thoughtful for a while before she said, "That's a noble sentiment, but I'm not sure I buy it."

Matt was startled. "What do you mean?"

She sighed. "Are you sure you haven't been using this tragedy as an excuse?"

"An excuse for what?"

"All sorts of things." Once again, she ticked off points on her fingers. "You've stayed lonely to punish yourself for the bad ones that got away. And for the innocent ones that didn't get away. To cultivate the image of a lone hunter. As an excuse not to settle down — because you believe you'd have to retire if you settled down. Or as an excuse not to grow up. I'm a cop myself, Matt. Believe me, I know the kind of psychological crap we can pull on ourselves."

"Woman, you sound like Marcus," he

blurted out in affront.

She chuckled. "Marc is not nearly as dumb as he looks."

Matt was flabbergasted and furious. "Do you have *any* clue how I've denied myself these last three years? The moment I saw you, I knew we were meant to be bonded. But I chose to walk away. I knew what could happen if I let the bond happen, but I chose to save you instead. It is a Prime's *duty* to protect the one he loves. I did it for you!"

"You — chose."

"Yes. It was the hardest thing I've ever done."

"I see."

She did not come rushing into his arms to soothe his pain. "Is there a bathroom in this place?" she asked, standing abruptly.

He was so taken aback that all he could manage was to point toward a hallway. "That way."

Phillipa nodded politely and stalked away.

Matt stared after her, totally confused at the turn the conversation had taken. What was she so angry about? What had he done?

He scratched his head. He considered nursing a rage at being offended. But when he heard the shower turn on, he decided that he'd already wasted too much time being without her in the last three years. They had to work this out right away.

Besides, the idea of confronting her when she was naked and slippery wet was irresistibly appealing.

CHAPTER
THIRTY-ONE

"There you are."

The vampire's voice was annoyingly pleasant as it opened the car door and slid into the passenger seat.

Michele was stopped at a red light on Las Vegas Boulevard, and the last thing she'd expected was to have the monster suddenly appear beside her car and gesture for her to unlock the door.

"What are you doing here?" she asked.

"Don't sound so annoyed," the vampire chided. "I'm the one who's been all over town looking for you."

"You could have thought to call me."

The vampire gave her a caustic look. "I do live in the twenty-first century. Your cell phone hasn't been on. What have you been doing all day?"

"Hunting a vampire," Michele answered. "You're telepathic, why didn't you call me that way?"

The light changed and she pressed on the gas pedal, and neon blurred past on either side. Sunset had changed the look of the street, and the Strip was now alight.

"Even I must conserve my energy sometimes. I have a big night planned." The vampire *tsk*ed. "Vampire hunting is not what I told you to do."

"The vampire is protecting the human you told us to kill. He's with her."

"Ah, well. That's different." The vampire patted her on the top of the head. "Good work, then. Where is this vampire?"

Michele frowned as she gave the creature a sideways glance. "If I knew, I wouldn't be driving in circles trying to pick up his trail."

"I see. You were following his car, but you lost sight of him."

"Yes. He stopped Andrew from killing the bitch, then I followed him when he tried to follow Andrew. He lost Andrew, but then I lost him."

"It's been a farcical waste of time, in other words."

Michele ground her teeth together in frustration. "Yes."

"That's all right, don't worry about it. It's up to Andrew to take care of the woman. I have another task for you and the others."

"But Andrew needs —"

"Andrew can take care of himself. Your duty is to do as I tell you." The vampire chuckled. "As I said, I have big plans for this evening, and I do not wish to be disturbed."

"And these plans are?" Michele asked, because it was obvious that the vampire was dying to tell her.

"I got the idea from *Ocean's Eleven* — the original, not the recent remake. And from your crew's caper, as well. I thought, Why not hit more than one place in a day? We've milked this as much as we can, and it's time to make a big score and get out. While I am doing that, your people will be diverting the only person who can stop us."

Michele stopped the car at another red light. "But —" she began, then suddenly felt as though the vampire was clutching her mind in a heavy fist.

"Don't argue with me," the monster said. "You're going to enjoy the job I have planned for you. You see, I know where the vampire and the bitch are hiding. I'm going to set up a diversion for you, and when they return from it, your crew will be set up to take them down. I'd rather that you didn't kill the vampire, but I suppose you deserve some reward for all the help you've given me. Now listen carefully."

The rest of the vampire's instructions were poured directly into Michele's head. She was exhausted and dizzy by the time the vampire left her mind, yet it had all happened by the time the red light changed to green.

The vampire said, "It's been nice working with you," opened the door, and stepped out. The last Michele saw of the creature, it was standing on the sidewalk, holding a cellular phone to its ear.

"Why doesn't Matt answer his phone?" Mike complained.

"Maybe he doesn't have an American calling plan," Jason suggested, coming back into the room after feeding the wolves. He tapped his forehead. "Why not try reaching him the old-fashioned way?"

"Because werefolk don't have the same kind of telepathy you do."

Mike put the phone down and sat on the dressing room couch as Jason began taking out costume pieces from his closet. When Cage turned around, Mike tapped the side of his nose. "This is our old-fashioned way. But you could send a thought your cousin's way for me —"

"Oh, no." Jason draped the costumes over the back of a chair. "There's no way I'm touching Bridger's mind. The Man and I don't exactly get along."

"Fine," Mike said, standing. "I guess I'll just have to sniff him out the regular way. Thanks for all your help —"

His words were interrupted by the ringing of the telephone. When Jason answered, Mike could hear that the voice on the other end was a woman's.

By the time she finished speaking, the vampire looked disappointed, but he answered cheerfully enough. "No problem. We'll make it some other night." He hung up with a frown.

"She broke your date, right?" Mike asked.

Cage nodded. "There are only two vampire females in Vegas, and Octavia's the only one not attached. Holding her attention is not easy."

"Better luck next time," Mike commiserated.

"Thanks."

"Well, I better get going."

"No, wait. I think I can help you."

Mike grinned. "I think you just like having wolves of any type around. How can you help?"

"I think I know where Bridger might be. There's a place we keep outside of town; Octavia probably set him up there. It's somewhere the Purists won't find him while he's looking for them. Wait until after my show, and I'll take you there." He gave a sardonic smile. "It's not like I have anything better to do this evening."

Though this meant waiting a couple more hours, Mike saw the sense of it. Who knew how many hours it would take him to track Bridger down, anyway? He might as well be comfortable while he waited.

"Okay," Mike said. "We'll do it your way — Beast Master."

CHAPTER
THIRTY-TWO

It is a Prime's duty to protect the one he loves.

Matt's words rang in her head, and Phillipa slapped her hand against the pale pink shower tiles.

"What the hell's a Prime anyway?" she muttered angrily. "Who the hell does he think he is? A prime idiot! A prime piece of —"

"May I join you?" Matt asked as he pulled back the shower curtain.

Her diatribe sputtered to a halt, and she glared. "You're naked."

"I've said something to upset you," was his response.

"You think?"

He stepped into the shower cubicle. It was barely big enough to hold the two of them, and heat shivered through her as warm, wet skin slid against hers. She quickly became aware of hard thighs against her buttocks and of the broad chest against her back. Hot steam rose around them, and it was suddenly flavored with his masculine scent. She couldn't help but tilt her head back against his shoulder and close her eyes, luxuriating in being surrounded by him. His arms came around her waist, and drew her even closer.

"Not fair," she complained.

"Are you under the mistaken impression that there are rules of engagement?"

He kissed her shoulder, then nipped at her earlobe. It was a good thing he was holding her, because her knees went weak.

"We're not at war," she told him.

"But we are in love." His breath was warm against her wet cheek. "All's fair in both, remember?"

Being told that he loved her was a balm to her anger, but it didn't bring instant forgiveness.

"People in love have problems," she told him.

"Problems can be corrected easily enough."

One of his hands slid slowly up to cup her breasts; the other moved down her belly and between her thighs. Skilled fingers teased and coaxed her into an absolute frenzy that drove away everything but need and pleasure. She swore at him, but he soon turned her to face him. He grasped her buttocks, lifted her, and slid his erection deeply inside her. Phillipa wrapped her legs around his hips and rode the storm while he pounded deliciously into her and water pounded over them.

After orgasms took them both, she said, "I'm still pissed as hell, Bridger."

"But you're clean and happy," he answered. "Sex and soap are the answer to many problems, my sweet." He reached around her and turned off the water.

Phillipa slipped past him out of the shower, but he moved fast, and blocked the bathroom door before she could get out. He held out a fluffy pink towel, rather like a matador waiting for a bull charge. But instead of shouting *Ole!* he proceeded to gently pat the water off her damp skin and hair. This was such a sensual pleasure that she closed her eyes and let him finish.

"Still angry?" he asked when he was done.

She tossed a towel his way, and didn't offer to return the favor. "Yes."

But she did watch appreciatively as Matt dried off his sturdy, hard-muscled body. When he was done, she began to dress, and noticed that a bruise on her stomach that had been large and purple the day before was almost gone.

"Interesting," she murmured, rubbing the

spot that was no longer sore.

Matt left to get dressed, and she soon finished and followed him. The scent of brewing coffee led her to the kitchen.

"Bless you," she said, when Matt handed her the first cup.

He ran a finger along her jawline. "You are most welcome, sweet. Now, please tell me what you think I've done."

She took a sip of coffee, then carefully set the cup on the counter to avoid the temptation of tossing it in his face.

"Choice," she said. "And the lack of it. *You* chose to ignore that we had a psychic connection. *You* chose to leave. You made all the choices."

"Of course. I am Prime."

"What the hell does that mean?"

His frustration was palpable. "It means a great many things, but in this case, it means that it was my duty to make the choice to protect you."

She crossed her arms, tightly balling her fists. "Can you understand how much what you've just said hurts me?"

"Hurts *and* angers," he replied. He pressed his fingers across his forehead. "Sweetness, you're projecting enough to give me a headache."

"Do *not* patronize me, Bridger. One more

sweetness, and I walk out of here."

He grinned. "But you don't know where we are."

"I'm the one who set the GPS," she reminded him. "I know exactly where we are."

He sighed. "So you did. I suppose I'm the one who is lost. Please tell me why you are angry with me."

"You. Gave. Me. No. Choices. You made the decisions without consulting me. Why don't you get that?"

"I —"

"Do you know what my life has been like in the last months? I had the life I loved, the life *I decided on,* taken away from me. Through no choice of my own! Just to stay alive, I've had to follow rules and regulations and regimens that doctors and shrinks and nutritionists and personnel departments and insurance companies decided for me.

"I live by numbers — what's my blood sugar? What's my blood pressure? How many cc's of insulin do I need? What's my A1C number? The numbers determine my life. I do what I'm told, and I don't feel in control of anything. Hell, my only act of defiance has been getting the tattoo, and even *then* I had to ask my doctor's permission. I'm told it'll get easier, but right now it's driving me crazy.

"Then you come along and tell me one more decision was taken out of my hands. That is why I am angry!" Her voice rose with each word, so that she was shouting by the time she finished.

He said quietly, "I am not going to apologize because you have diabetes."

She threw up her hands. "That isn't the point!"

"It is one of the points."

He came closer, and she backed away. When he finally had her in a corner between cabinets and the sink, he put his hands on her shoulders. She was shaking.

"Three years ago, I couldn't explain to you what I am, and who I am, and how it affects *us.*"

"You could have!"

"*Maybe* I could have confessed all to you that night," he conceded. "But I didn't think bonding was safe for my partner. I am *still* terrified that I can't keep you safe. But now I accept that what is between us is right, and inevitable. I didn't then. When I chose to leave you, I acted on what I believed was best for you then. I knew it wasn't good for me — I've missed you every moment we've been apart."

He still didn't get it. Phillipa was aware of the genuine pain and regret he felt for the time they'd spent apart. But he was clueless why she was so angry.

Hollering had helped; she was calmer now. So she tried again, in a more reasonable tone. "You left me out of the decision-making process. You didn't ask me what *I* wanted."

He closed his eyes for a moment. "All right," he said when he opened them. "Point taken. What do *you* want?"

"I want a partner, not a lord and master."

"Oh, dear, I was afraid it was something like that." His answer was couched in a very snooty British accent.

"Don't make me laugh, you rat bastard. This is serious stuff." She managed not to laugh, but she couldn't keep a brief smile from her lips.

"You are so lovely," he told her.

"And you're trying to distract me," she told him.

"Guilty as charged, Officer Elliot." He leaned close and kissed her forehead, then her temple.

She couldn't help but sigh, and very nearly melted at his gentle touch. It was very hard to stay furious, or even focused, when simply being close to him kept her on the edge of desire.

She started to put her arms around him, but stopped dead cold when he whispered, "You don't have to worry about the disease anymore. Not while you share my blood."

What was he talking about? What did he mean?

But the telephone in the living room rang before she could ask, and Matt immediately went to answer it.

Phillipa stared after him, too flabbergasted to move. His voice seemed to come from a great distance away. Her whole world had been thrown into a tailspin.

"If you share blood with a vampire, that'll cure it."

That was what Marcus had said.

"It's not possible," she murmured. "It simply is not possible."

"What isn't?" Matt asked, coming back into the kitchen. "Time to roll, partner," he added before she could answer. "We've got a location on the man who's been trying to kill you."

295

CHAPTER
THIRTY-THREE

"I need to go back to my car," she said.

Phillipa stared out the windshield as the lights of the city grew closer by the second. She held on tightly to the panic that tried to erupt in her brain while her stomach twisted with nervous terror.

"I need my purse," she told Matt. "I left my purse in my car." She had her keys and her phone, but everything really important was in her purse.

"If you want a gun, there's a twenty-two in the glove box."

That was nice to know, but a gun wasn't what she wanted. "I'd prefer the one locked in my car trunk."

She didn't actually care if she had a gun or not. She needed the stuff in her purse. "I need to check my blood glucose level." She needed her insulin pen and the needles that went with it. She could only hope that the insulated cool pack the medication was stored in had kept the insulin mixture from going bad through the heat of the day. And since she took her blood pressure medications in the evening, she also needed the pill case that was in her purse.

"I need my stuff."

You had to be consistent about treating the disease; you needed to stick to a routine. You needed to pay attention, prepare for emergencies. It was *important.*

"Phillipa, what is the matter with you?"

That was a very good question. She had stopped thinking, and after all these months of being so careful.

"My blood sugar must be through the roof. Or maybe it's getting too low. I need to check my numbers and figure out what to do from there."

"You don't need to check anything." He reached over and squeezed her hand. "You are fine," he assured her confidently. "Now, concentrate on the op. I need you on your game, Officer."

She knew she wasn't fine. She *couldn't* be fine. Who was she to be fine? Matt couldn't understand. How could he? He probably couldn't even get sick. That was okay. It was her responsibility to manage it and keep it under control.

But he was right. She needed to concentrate on the job. Having a panic attack wasn't going to help them get through a potentially dangerous situation. This guy had to be brought down, for Jo and Brandon's sake.

Then she'd get her stuff.

She straightened up in her seat and took a few deep, steadying breaths. "Where are we going? Is this guy alone or with the rest of his gang? Where'd you get your intel, and can you trust it? Do we have backup?"

"The call was from Octavia," Matt replied. He smiled when a sideways glance her way showed that she was frowning at the name. "Octavia is the one who set up surveillance on our target, after we found out that he works in one of the casinos around Fremont Street. After shooting at us, he was spotted entering his place of employment."

"Vampire hunting isn't a full-time occupation?"

"Once upon a time it was, but most of the time there is a truce between hunters and supernatural folk these days. The Families and Clans police our own, and we also help the hunters keep the Tribes in check. The hunters don't like us, but they don't kill us anymore. Except every now and then a faction of hunters called the Purists pull some stupid move."

"The who? The what?"

"The Purists broke the truce when they went after Marcus's family," he went on without offering any more detailed explanations. "And the Purist we're after will be getting off work soon. You and I are going to put him out of business."

Phillipa stood in the middle of the roofed-over street and looked up at the pretty lights that arched overhead. The light show shifted in psychedelic patterns as a Jimi Hendrix song played on the sound system. Fremont Street was lined on either side with some of the city's older casinos. Closed to traffic, it was crowded with people, most of whom had stopped to gawk at the multimedia show that was the area's main tourist draw. Phillipa liked this part of town a lot, although she'd never entered any of the casinos that used the light show to lure customers away from the swankier establishments lining the Las Vegas Strip.

While she enjoyed the show, she was very aware of the time. She checked her watch once more and began walking up the street. She'd done some undercover work hunting for a killer who preyed on prostitutes, and now she automatically moved in the hooker's stroll she'd learned on that assignment.

Though she appeared casual, she was alert for any signs that she was being followed.

She walked all the way up the several blocks under the glittering lights and was nearly back to her starting point when she spotted her prey. Once she knew she was being followed, she headed toward the shadows of the streets beyond the casinos. He caught up to her when she reached a parking lot where no one was around.

"It *is* you!" the Purist declared when she turned to face him.

"It sure is," she answered, bringing up the small gun she'd taken from her waistband. "On your knees," she directed. "And put your hands behind your head."

Matt hated standing by and watching this takedown, but he had to admire his woman's professionalism as she turned and raised her weapon. He'd been closely following the man who followed her, prepared for danger yet worried about having her play decoy. Watching her hip-swaying walk as she lured the Purist into the trap had certainly been arousing, though.

Even more arousing was her sheer, dangerous competence. He was Prime, and his impulse was to protect his mate, but he knew that his mate needed this. Besides, it was her right as Brandon's guardian. It was what his supernatural enemies could do to the woman he loved that he feared. The man kneeling before her now was a mere mortal.

Matt came up behind the Purist. "Good work, sweet."

The man's head jerked around. "You!"

He started to rise, but Matt put his hand on the top of the Purist's head and held him down. "I'll take it from here," he told Phillipa.

"What now?" she asked. She reached for her mobile phone. "Should I call LVPD?"

"No," Matt and the Purist said at the same time.

"That isn't how this game is played," Matt went on.

"You've corrupted her," the Purist claimed. "You creatures destroy all that's pure. I have to kill her. My orders are to kill her." He looked at Phillipa and started crying. "I hate that I have to kill her."

Phillipa looked worriedly at Matt. "He's pretty pathetic. You aren't going to hurt him, are you?"

Matt didn't point out that she was the one holding the gun on the man at her feet. "Don't you want revenge?"

She sighed. "Maybe if someone had actually been hurt. They attacked a baby, after all. Brandon and Jo deserve justice, but justice isn't the same as revenge."

He smiled. "I knew you were going to say that."

"What I want is for him to leave my family alone. Him and all his friends."

"I totally agree," Matt answered.

"If we can't turn him in to the police, couldn't he just forget about us?"

Matt nodded. "That is how the game is played. Give me a moment."

Had Phillipa not been standing there, Matt might have punished the Purist a bit, but since beating the shit out of the mortal wasn't the sort of civilized behavior befitting being in the presence of his love, Matt forsook the pleasure.

Once inside the Purist's head, he quickly decided that the man was far too pathetic to warrant anything but a quick mind-wipe. Yet there was something very disturbing about the man's mind. There was a touch of more than one personality there, and one of them wasn't mortal. Matt probed deeper, looking for answers, information, identities. He found very little, but what he *did* find he didn't like.

When he was done, the Purist got up and ran. Matt looked around to tell Phillipa that she was safe from this one now, but she was nowhere to be seen.

For a moment he was terrified that something had happened to her, but the fear quickly passed. She was his mate: he could find her in heaven, hell, and anywhere on earth. Besides, he was already certain where she had gone. All he had to do was follow.

Chapter
Thirty-Four

Phillipa sat in her parked car and held up her hands. With stunned numbness, she studied her fingers in the light of a streetlamp. Each dot of blood, and the scar tissue forming beneath it, represented a pinprick. They represented all the times she had tested her blood glucose level in the last several months.

The most recent pinprick still stung a little, since she'd tested her blood glucose as soon as the cab dropped her off by her car. She couldn't believe what the meter reading told her. And it couldn't be true that there weren't as many marks on her fingers as she remembered. There had to be something wrong with the equipment, and with her perceptions. This was too good to be true.

She shook her head. "I'm going crazy."

She wasn't surprised when Matt opened her door and pulled her out to stand next to the car. He put his hands on her waist. "No, you're not," he replied.

"What would you know about it?" She put her arms around him and leaned her head wearily on his shoulder. "You're a vampire."

He drew her close. "Being a vampire makes it easier for me to spot crazy people. It's a gift — along with my amazing sexual prowess."

She laughed softly, but couldn't deny his claim about being good in bed. "You know what I've always been good at?"

"What?"

"I've always been able to spot the bad guys. That's why I haven't had screaming hysterics about falling for a blood-sucking monster."

"I'll thank you not to refer to us as monsters. Such language would upset my mother if she were here. You *are* on the verge of hysterics, though," he added. "Why, I can't fathom."

"You've never been sick, have you?"

"I've been wounded badly enough that it took a while to recover, but no, I have no concept of what illness must be like. And you don't have to worry about it anymore, sweetheart, please believe that."

The world had shifted a lot beneath her feet in the last few days, but this last change

305

jolted her the hardest. That the supernatural world existed — she could deal with that. That she was finally together with the man who was meant for her — she rejoiced in that. That her sister and nephew were no longer being threatened — that proved she could still do her job.

All these things had shaken her, but everything was turning out okay. But this . . . this . . .

"I don't deserve a miracle."

Matt silently held her for a while, and she took comfort from being folded in his embrace. "I think the point about miracles is that no one *deserves* them," he said finally. "Miracles are gifts; they simply occur. But I'm not offering you a miracle," he added. "I'm simply offering you *me* — just my bad-tempered, stubborn, high-handed, difficult-to-live-with, don't-ask-me-to-help-with-the-laundry self."

She looked into his face. "You are my miracle." Anguish almost choked her, but it was laced with joy, even if it was a guilty joy. "Over twenty-one million people in America have diabetes. And those are just the ones who know they have it. It's a cause of heart disease and kidney failure and blindness, and most limb amputations are diabetes-related. Why am *I* the one who gets to walk away from this killer? It's not fair or right that I'm the one person in the world who gets to be cured."

"No," Matt agreed. "It is not fair. Are you under any illusion that life is fair?"

She shook her head. "But don't you see how confusing this is? How hard this is? Can you fix anyone else?"

"No."

"Do I love you because you can make it better? It terrifies me that maybe it isn't *you* I love — that maybe I sensed somehow that you could cure me, and that's what drew me to you. You deserve more than a woman who wants to use you."

"Yes, I certainly do." He put a finger over her lips. "Or maybe I love you because you're diabetic. I have a terrible sweet tooth, after all."

That made her smile.

"Neither of us knew you were ill when we met, did we?" he asked. She shook her head. "It was lust at first sight, wasn't it?"

Phillipa nodded, and her smile turned into a wicked grin.

"What we share, the blending of our blood and psychic energy, will extend your life." He gave a crooked smile. "And it will complete mine."

She touched his cheek. "Mine, too."

"I concede that you were right in suggesting I was punishing myself with loneliness," he went on. "I can't apologize for not consulting you about fighting the bonding, but I do see your point about wanting choices."

"Lack of apology accepted," she told him. "Just don't *not* consult me about something that concerns both of us again."

"Very well, my love. From now on, I'll ask your opinion before we do it my way."

She chose to laugh rather than argue — for now. She was under no illusions that what they had would be a partnership, but she also doubted that there would be many things that they disagreed on. They were, after all, bondmates.

"I'm still terrified of something happening to you," Matt said. "But not enough to try to run away from what we have. Please don't punish yourself by believing you don't deserve this gift of health I can give you." He patted her rump. "And don't consider it a gift, because I'm going to work your fanny off for it."

"Really?" she asked, and pressed her pelvis against his. She felt him harden against her.

He closed his eyes. "Woman, do you want me to take you here against the car?"

"Hell, no," she answered. "Not when

there's a perfectly good bed back at the house."

He put a finger under her chin. "Are you going to be all right?"

She thought about it. It *wasn't* right, or fair, but he was correct about life not being fair. It was wonderful.

"I'll adapt," she told him. "I have to, because I am not losing you."

CHAPTER
THIRTY-FIVE

"How did you find out about this place?" Britney asked.

Michele was really getting tired of the younger woman's questions.

"Are you sure this thing will work?" Britney went on.

"Yes. And it's called a zapper." Michele knelt in front of the small device she'd set in the middle of the living room, and checked the output readings once more. "It's been used quite effectively in San Diego. One of my nephews designed it," she added proudly. "He's made quite a lot of improvements lately. This version draws power from a small lithium battery; the original versions weren't as compact and portable."

Britney, of course, was not impressed. "But do they actually work? Our lives might depend on that thing working."

"You are such a Luddite," Kevin said

to Britney.

"What's that?" Britney asked.

Kevin just shook his head, and went back to staring out the living room window.

Michele was glad he was sufficiently recovered from being stabbed with a knitting needle to join them. She was equally glad that he'd brought along his brother Doug, since Andrew was absent, and the other local Purist had quit the group when the operation to kill the brat went sour.

They'd broken into the vampire's hidden lair an hour before and set up shop in the dark house. When you hunted vampires, you got used to working in ambient light. Doug was outside watching the road; Kevin had his post by the window. The waiting was making them all nervous. Michele *so* wanted to get this over with. She was weary of the hunt, and very nervous about why she was involved. The younger hunters were driving her crazy. And the vampire — no, she mustn't think about the vampire.

"He means that you're afraid of innovation," Michele explained to Britney.

Britney held up a small canister of garlic spray. "I know this works. And I know silver works against the bastards, and wood."

She carried a slender wooden dagger; Kevin was armed with a specially modified gun that shot silver bullets.

Britney nudged the zapper with her foot. "This — I don't know what this does."

"I've already explained. It creates an energy field that dampens the vampire's psychic abilities. This will keep them from detecting our presence."

"Until it's too late," Kevin added. "Now, if they'd only get here. I'd like to get the job over with and go home."

"Yes. Let's get it over with once and for all and strike a blow for humanity," Britney said with fierce pleasure. "I've been waiting to destroy the vampire race my entire life."

"One at a time." Kevin suddenly tensed. "I think I see lights approaching."

Michele shot to her feet and motioned to Britney. "By the door," she ordered. She drew out a silver dagger, and crouched tensely behind the couch.

"Slow down. Something's wrong," Mike said.

He leaned forward in his seat and took deep breaths. The wolves in the backseat did the same. Cage was driving a convertible, and Mike had been enjoying drinking in the night air.

Jason braked to a crawl on the rutted dirt

road. "I never argue with a werewolf's nose. What is it, boy?"

"Don't call me —"

"I was talking to George," the vampire hastily informed him.

Mike didn't buy that, but he let it go. Why argue with a guy who played with lions and tigers?

"It's not so much what I scent, but . . . Mortals came this way recently. Matt's also been here."

With a woman, Mike could tell, detecting the musk and psychic residue of sex even a quarter mile away from the house. He recognized the scent of the woman Matt had been with back at the hotel. At least now he knew why his friend had kept his phone off. The perfect woman, Matt had called her. Mike guessed Matt Bridger had gotten over his fear of settling down.

"But Bridger isn't here now," Jason said. "I don't detect his presence, either."

So they wouldn't be interrupting the honeymoon. It was certainly better to wait for his return than to interrupt a vampire in heat. Even so, Mike didn't like the feel of the area. There was an absence up ahead, a hole in the fabric of the universe that tickled his senses. He couldn't quite put his finger on it, but there was something familiar about what he wasn't feeling.

"What do you detect?" he asked the vampire.

"Not a damn thing," Jason replied. He stopped the car. "That's not good, is it?"

Mike finally recognized the psychic absence up ahead. Besides, he could now detect the faintest humming sound. Glancing into the backseat, he saw that the wolves' ears were pricked at the sound.

"Zapper. It's an antivampire device," he explained. "It was invented by the brother of an ex-vampire hunter who works in my family's detective agency."

"An *ex*-vampire hunter?"

"Yeah. She hooked up with a Tribe Prime, but he reformed, and they had a baby and now they both work with us. What can I say? Good help is hard to find."

"I still don't get it, but we don't have the time to gossip right now."

"Not when there's an ambush waiting for us up ahead."

The vampire grinned, showing very sharp teeth. "It looks like this evening is going to be entertaining, after all. How do you want to handle it?"

Mike began to take off his borrowed clothes. "I think you should drive up to the house and spring the trap." He jumped out of the car. "Okay if I take Burns and Allen with me?"

CHAPTER THIRTY-SIX

"That was a gunshot!" Phillipa said.

"It most certainly was," Matt answered.

"What was *that?*" she asked about the eerie sound that followed the gunfire.

"Werewolf." Matt flipped off the car lights and floored the gas pedal.

They'd had the windows down to enjoy the night air, and he'd just made the last turn to the safe house when the crack of sound came out of the night.

Phillipa gave him a sharp look. "Werewolf?" She surprised him by saying, "So there really *is* a werewolf responsible for the killings Pete's investigating."

He frowned at the mention of her police detective friend. "Yes."

"You know about that?" She sounded outraged.

"Don't take that tone, woman. I *am* a vampire cop. My partner, Mike Bleythin, is in town looking into the lycanthrope matter."

316

"Your partner? You said you worked alone."

"No, I said that only a single vampire does my job at a time. Mike's the werewolf copper."

Another howl sounded as they drew closer to the house.

"And that sounds like him now."

Another pair of howls sounded from different directions.

"Those sound like real wolves," Phillipa said. "George and Gracie?"

Matt was confused for a moment, then he remembered. "Jason Cage's wolves. What's Mike doing with Cage?"

"More importantly, why are shots coming from your safe house?"

"That *is* the most important point," he agreed.

He stopped the car behind the cover of a bush, and fought the urge to order her to stay put. Anyway, she was out of the car almost before he shifted to park. Since he could move much faster than Phillipa, he grabbed her before she'd gone more than a step.

"I'm the one who gets to rush headlong into danger. You bring the gun and follow as backup."

"Okay," she conceded. "But — there's a

werewolf, and real wolves and unknown suspects. How do I know who to shoot?"

He brushed a finger reassuringly across her cheek. "That's simple. You always know who the bad guys are, right?"

Phillipa moved cautiously by moonlight across the sandy, uneven ground, her gun held stiffly before her. The house was a low one-story bulk ahead of her. She could hear movement and people shouting, as well as occasional gunfire and animals growling.

A couple of days ago this weirdness would have shaken her, but now she took it in stride. *Just another day at the office.* She grinned.

As she approached the opened front door the living room lights were switched on, temporarily blinding her.

As her eyes adjusted, she heard Jason Cage say, "That was fun; let's do it again."

"Let's not." Matt's voice cut across a sound she could only describe as a dog laughing.

Or more likely a wolf, she supposed. No, it had to be the werewolf because she saw the real wolves standing on either side of the front porch as if on guard.

"Phillipa!" Matt called from the doorway.

"Matthias," she called back to her bondmate. "Is it clear?"

"Come inside," he answered.

A huge black wolf came past her when she went through the open front door, and she watched the animal trot into the darkness before she entered the crowded living room, closing the door behind her.

"Hello, again," Jason Cage said with a delighted smile as she came in.

"Oh, stop it."

He stood on one side of the room and Matt on the other, but they gave the impression of having the bad guys surrounded. She was beginning to understand that this sort of macho jockeying and posturing was typical Prime interplay, and she ignored them. She concentrated her attention on the two men and two women crowded together in the center of the room, holding her weapon steadily on them.

One of the women was young, her eyes full of hatred as she glanced between the two vampires. The two men looked tense and scared. The other woman was somewhere on the edge of elderly, but fit, with short gray hair and a calm, alert demeanor. She was obviously the brains of the operation, and she looked vaguely familiar.

"You're the ones who attacked my family," Phillipa accused. "Why were you trying to hurt a baby?"

"That brat's an abomination," the younger woman spat out. She glared at Phillipa. "You should be dead, you filthy whore."

Phillipa had heard far worse insults from much nastier perps. Unimpressed, she looked at Matt. "Now what?"

The front door opened again, and Phillipa turned her gun on a tall, black-haired man who was buttoning a white shirt as he entered. He stopped and quickly put his hands in the air, but he was grinning.

"That's Mike Bleythin," Matt told her.

She remembered the huge black beast that had gone out as she came in, and realized the big, dark man with the half-open shirt was the werewolf returning in human form. He must have gone outside to change — in more ways than one.

"Nice to meet you, Mike." She shifted the gun back toward the prisoners.

"Your lady's a cop, isn't she?" Mike asked. "You didn't mention that when you told me about her."

"We'll discuss my lady later," Matt said to Mike. "What are you doing here? With him?" He tilted his head toward Cage.

Cage put a hand on his heart and said snidely, "We were attempting to come to your rescue, cousin."

Matt sneered briefly at Cage. "No, really," he said to Mike.

"While I was looking for you, we ran into a Purist ambush," Mike answered. "I was looking for you because we have business together: tracker and guardian business."

"What about your renegade lycanthrope?"

"I found my lycanthrope, but one of yours gave me some trouble. Jason has been a great deal of help with the case, so play nice with your cousin."

"What do you mean, one of *mine?*"

Mike sighed. "I'm trying to obliquely tell you that there's some vampire bad guys roaming the streets."

"Some?" Matt asked. "The bank robbers."

"The bank robbers are vampires?" Phillipa asked at the same time.

"At least two vampires, and the lycanthrope," Mike said.

"One of the bad vampires messed with Mike's mind," Jason spoke up. "And you and I both know the penalties for that sort of telepathic tampering."

Phillipa noted that the three supernatural types didn't seem particularly concerned about their human prisoners. The older woman was looking annoyed, and Phillipa almost didn't blame her.

"What about these guys?" she asked.

"What are they doing here? What happens to them now?"

Matt finally turned his attention to the Purists. "What happens to them? We do some tampering of our own."

"Like you did with Andrew?" Phillipa asked.

Her bondmate nodded.

Phillipa sighed with relief, glad that she wasn't going to have to defend a bunch of scummy humans from the Prime she loved. It wasn't that she didn't instinctively trust Matthias — but this idea of vampire justice was new to her. She was going to have to study the legal codes of the supernatural world as soon as she got the chance.

"What have you done to Andrew, you monster?" the younger woman demanded.

"What I'm about to do to you," Matt said, and stepped toward her.

Matt hated this part of the job. He'd already been inside one mortal's head this evening; now he was stuck with four more ignorant minds to obscure. This was the most he'd ever had to deal with at any one time. He was already exhausted, and all he wanted was to spend time with his woman. But from what he'd just learned, it looked that dealing with the Purists was only the beginning of the operation. What he needed was an apprentice — or at least someone that could be of some help.

He glanced sourly at Jason Cage. *You're a strong telepath. Make yourself useful, Jason of House Ioana,* he thought at the former fugitive. *Work on the two males,* he ordered before Cage could argue. He grabbed the younger woman's hand even as she tried to dodge away.

He had to cut through layers of hatred and vitriol, along with deep terror, before he could make her believe that she had no interest in killing anyone, especially vampires from the Families or Clans. At least not for the next year or two.

The temptation was always to make the fanatics completely forget everything they knew about vampires, but altering of basic personality was not only forbidden, it was almost impossible to do, especially without driving the subject insane.

It didn't take long to convince the girl to change, but his head was aching by the time he was finished. He rubbed his forehead, gave Phillipa a reassuring smile, and turned to the older woman.

Her terror was a silent, rising scream as he approached, yet she stared daggers at him. She was proud, and stubborn, and had been hating vampires for a long time. He could tell that she was going to be a hard case even before he touched her.

You can't know! She shouted into his mind. *It doesn't want you to know!*

He knew instantly that the poor woman had been mind-raped by a vampire.

So what he had to do now was far more delicate work. The victim had to be treated gently. This time it was permitted to take away the memories of what had been done, but he had to search them out and learn the whole truth before he could finally give the woman peace.

When he was finished, he handed the woman over to her friends and told them all, "Go!"

When the mortals were out of the house, he looked at Phillipa, Mike, and Jason. They were all staring at him expectantly.

"It's Octavia," he said. "Octavia has been using the Purists. She set everyone up."

CHAPTER THIRTY-SEVEN

"It can't be Octavia," Jason objected. "I'm dating her."

"Hey, she stood you up tonight," Mike pointed out.

"She's the bad guy?" Phillipa said. "So *that's* why I've never liked her. I thought I was just jealous."

"But Octavia was rescued from having to live as a Tribe female," Jason went on. "She has all the respect and status due a matri. Why would she —"

"Maybe she's just bad," Mike interrupted. "The vampire female that took me down loved using her power. I know the Families disapprove of that sort of behavior. And I remember that she had absolutely no respect for humans," he added. "That explains why she wouldn't have any scruples about using them."

"Or stealing from them," Phillipa put in. "Does the use of telepathy explain how they pulled off their jobs? I remember seeing a street surveillance tape on the news that showed police surrounding the robbery crew. The police all looked stunned, and they got away. You were there," she added to Mike.

"I was following my nose and walked into trouble," he told her. "The cops shot me instead of the feral bastard I'm after."

"Are you all right?"

"Jason fixed me."

Matt listened to all this while he waited for the brutal headache from mind-touching all the mortals to fade. He'd discovered that a great deal had gone on recently that he needed to know about.

But there was one thing he knew for sure.

He looked at Phillipa. "We've only been together for a few days, and you've already been attacked by a vampire."

He saw that she was aware of his concern, but lifted her head defiantly. "I'm still standing," she told him.

"Because Octavia had flawed minions."

She tucked the gun in her belt and crossed her arms. "Because I have *you*," she said. "We're a team. We can take on anything."

He only wished he could believe that. "What about the next time?"

She shrugged. "What about it? Life isn't

safe. Who was it who reminded me that it also isn't fair?"

"How about you two save this for later, and we take out Octavia and the lycanthrope right now?" Mike spoke up.

"I don't know, Mike," Jason said. "I'm kind of looking forward to this fight."

Matthias spared both his friend and his cousin annoyed looks, but he had to agree with Mike. "Business first," he agreed.

"Yes," Phillipa said, "business first. Where do we find this vampire mastermind?"

"No," Matt answered adamantly. He shook his head at Phillipa. "I will allow you to help deal with mortals, but —"

The energy level in the room went up like a rocket. "You'll *allow?*" she shouted.

"It looks like we might get an entertaining fight after all," Jason said.

"You are not as amusing as you think you are," Matt informed the younger vampire, who merely smiled and shrugged at his words.

"But you have your uses." Matt gestured toward Phillipa, whose eyes were full of the light of battle, and couched his words as a formal request. "Jason of House Ioana, will you honor me by protecting my bondmate in my absence?"

Jason frowned. "If you put it that way, I

327

can't seduce her while you're gone."

"I'm standing right here!" Phillipa exclaimed. "And nobody is seducing me —"

"Let's go, Mike." Matt went to Phillipa and gave her a swift, hard kiss while she sputtered in indignation. Then he was out the door too swiftly for her to protest further. It pleased him that he had the taste of her on his lips as he went into battle.

"Are you going to let him get away with that?" Jason asked when Matt and Mike disappeared into the darkness.

Phillipa had turned toward the door to follow them, but the vampire's question stopped her, and she looked at him. He was smiling.

"Yes, I am suggesting a small rebellion against your autocratic beloved."

She was puzzled, but pleased at this turn of events. "Aren't you supposed to be guarding me?"

"Technically, I didn't actually agree to his request."

"Matthias did make an assumption," she agreed.

"Besides, I don't want to miss out on the fun any more than you do."

She was beginning to like this cousin of Matt's. Maybe she could get Jason to explain the animosity between them on the way into Las Vegas.

"Okay," she said. "Let's go." She knew she could sense her way to Matt wherever he went.

"My guess is that she arranged tonight's ambush as a diversion for you," Mike said as Matt drove.

"I know she did," Matt answered. "Octavia revealed her plan to the Purist leader, but there was nothing the mortal woman could do but set up the ambush, even though a part of her was fighting the control. Octavia didn't care if those mortals were driven mad, or killed. She didn't care if we were killed, as long as she got what she wanted out of the evening."

"Which is?" Mike enquired.

"She's hitting major casinos. She's doing it all for greed."

"And because she can," Mike added. "When she messed with my head, I was hit hard by the size of her ego." He breathed deeply, and swore. "My lycanthrope is hanging with your vampires. Why is it that your kind are always leading my kind astray?"

Matt snickered. "I believe you once told me that your kind are sly and clever, and use my kind's psychic energy to mask their presence from you. This means that your target is sticking close to my target this evening."

"I assume you have a pretty good idea of where they are."

Matt nodded. "She planned tonight as her gang's last score. While the local police are searching the city for her crew, the other vampires will be long gone. Octavia will be at home packing. I can't imagine her being the sort to travel light."

"I hope my boy's with her," Mike said. "It's likely, since crazy werewolves tend to accept crazy vampires as their pack alphas." He began to unbutton his shirt. "Time to double-team them."

CHAPTER
THIRTY-EIGHT

Being back in his wolf form for the second time this evening made Mike a little nervous. He was reassured by the knowledge that he could morph back to human whenever he wanted to, but as he approached the vampire's house, his awareness of the one who'd trapped him in wolf form grew stronger.

She was in there, all right. There was a knot of fear around his heart, fear that she would work her dark magic on him again.

It was embarrassing how spooked she had him.

But he was also angry enough to ignore the scared pup inside him that wanted to run away from the fight. He was angry enough to wish that Octavia was his prey tonight. Revenge would be sweet — but he'd come to town to hunt down a man-killer.

He cautiously circled the house, knowing

that the vampire's incredibly strong psychic field masked his presence from the other werewolf. At least the female was good for something.

There were lights on at the back, so he approached a window and spotted two figures standing in a large bedroom. He recognized one as his quarry. The pair were arguing. Mike didn't try to make out their conversation, but was delighted that their attention was intensely directed at each other.

Showtime, he thought, baring his fangs. He ran forward, and glass shattered as he leapt through the window into the bedroom, straight at the other werewolf.

He caught a flash of movement as the lycanthrope began to morph.

The vampire shouted, "Oh, no you don't!" *I've got you!*

Then her mind bored into his, and the world began to slow down and go dark.

Who has who, Octavia? Matt stepped into the room, his thoughts coming down like a net around her.

Though neither of them moved, mentally she turned to face him, and she was smiling. He heard vicious snarling and snapping as the two werewolves were freed to clash

332

with each other. While Mike did his job, Matt confronted his own enemy.

I've been looking forward to this, Octavia told him.

Her power probed at his defenses, like little flashes of lightning striking at his mind.

Why?

I am Tribe! she proudly told him. *The Families are weak. The Clans are pathetic. If my tribe hadn't given up the old ways, I'd be ruling the world by now.*

You'd be a slave in a Prime's harem, he answered. *Like any other Tribe female.*

Her laughter filled his soul. *Oh, I might be in a harem, but my lord and master would be the puppet I used to do whatever I wanted. I hate your rules. I hate pretending to be civilized. I'm going to crush you, Matthias, and then I'm going to do whatever I want.*

Really? He was probing her defenses as well. Her shielding was amazing. They'd been lovers once; why hadn't he detected her abilities when they'd shared blood and bodies?

I only made love to you to learn how your mind works, Octavia answered the thoughts he hadn't meant to share. *I learned your weaknesses, and the things you fear. I know how to defeat you, Guardian.*

How do you plan to do that?

Like this.

Her laughter ran through him like a rush of freezing floodwater. And he drowned in it. Lightning followed, searing him down to ash.

Matt couldn't see. He couldn't breathe. He couldn't think.

He woke up on a soft bed, with a terrible headache. Cool fingers brushed the hair from his forehead.

"You've had quite a night," Phillipa said. As he opened his eyes, she bent forward to kiss his forehead. He noticed her round breasts as her blouse gaped open, and every bit of pain faded at this lovely sight.

"Don't leer at me like that," she said as she stood. "I'm busy right now."

She crossed their bedroom to sit in the chair tucked into the curve of the bay window, and smiled at him as she picked up her knitting. He sat up on the side of the bed and watched her. He loved the pleasure her hobby gave her. He reveled in their being together, safe, at home.

Then the window shattered and the door burst open and dark shadows rushed in, eyes aglow, fangs dripping blood. They came for Phillipa.

He sat there frozen, dying inside, knowing he couldn't stop them.

Phillipa kept on knitting but briefly glanced his way and said, "Would you mind taking care of this? I have to count every stitch in this row if I'm going to get it right."

Her trust in him was all he needed.

Octavia, please, he told the vampire mucking with his head. *Is that the best you've got?*

Matt rose to his feet, and proceeded to twist the world back the way he wanted it.

"Good lord," Phillipa said as she walked into the bedroom, Jason a step behind her.

The first thing she saw was Matt and Octavia facing each other, eyes glazed over. They were as still as statues, yet clearly a struggle was going on between them.

Then the smell of death hit her, and her gaze went to a naked Mike Bleythin just as he finished morphing back into his human form. He wiped blood off his mouth with the back of his hand, and she saw the body lying on the floor with its throat torn out.

She was used to crime scenes, but this was the weirdest one she'd ever encountered. She turned her attention back to the vampires. She caught the impression of the pair being at the still center of a dangerous, twisting maelstrom. It made her sick and frightened to watch.

When she started toward Matt, Jason

grabbed her arm. "No," he whispered.

"What's happening?" she whispered back. "What's going on?"

"He's showing her why he's the most dangerous Prime in the Families," Jason answered. "When it comes down to it, it's not physical prowess that sets any of us apart from the others of our kind. We all have fangs and claws; we all have speed and agility and heightened senses. But it's the one with the strongest will and the finest telepathic skill that wins the real fights. Matthias is the Guardian because his mind is the strongest. Watch. Wait."

She did both anxiously, since there was nothing else she could do. He was doing battle in a place where she couldn't go, and she finally understood why he'd been so adamant about her staying out of his confrontation with Octavia.

It seemed like hours, but she doubted it was more than a few seconds before Octavia's eyes rolled back in her head, and she crumpled in a limp heap on the floor.

Matt didn't move for several more seconds. Then a massive shudder went through him. He gasped, and blinked, and rounded on her.

"What the devil are you doing here, woman?"

Phillipa reacted to his angry shout by rushing joyfully into his arms.

"You're right," she told him swiftly. "I shouldn't be here. From now on I'll stay out of the supernatural takedowns and only work with you on the human stuff."

"What makes you think I'm going to allow you to work with me at —" He got his temper under control, laughed, and hugged her tighter. "As if I could stop you."

He kissed her, and she felt him coming all the way back from a great distance as their mouths pressed hungrily to each other.

You make me live, he told her. *Be with me forever.*

Forever, she responded. *I promise.*

A hand touched her shoulder. "Guys," Mike said. "Our work here isn't finished yet."

She recalled that there was a dead body in the room, and quickly stepped away from Matt. She looked at Octavia. Jason was kneeling beside her.

"What'll happen to her?" she asked.

"She'll do hard time," Jason said, and there was a haunted look in his eyes. "But being a female of breeding age, it won't be all that hard on her, will it, Matthias?" he added bitterly.

"The sentence isn't up to me, Jason,"

Matt answered. "It never is. She might have gotten away with it for much longer," he added. "If she hadn't believed my being here could not be a coincidence."

As Jason picked Octavia up, Matt glanced at Mike, who nodded. He would leave his werewolf partner to deal with his own kind. The mortal police would never know what had happened here.

"Time for us to go," he said to Phillipa. "I still have another pair of vampires to hunt down. After this case is squared away, the two of us are going to have a long honeymoon somewhere where no one can interrupt us."

"That sounds nice," she answered. "And after the honeymoon, we can have a big, expensive wedding."

EPILOGUE

Four months later

"My in-laws are scary."

Phillipa arched a beautifully shaped eyebrow at Matt's pronouncement, and put her arm through his. She thought he looked incredibly handsome in a tuxedo. She was wearing a slinky white satin wedding dress.

"Maybe Mom is a little scary," she conceded. "She hasn't yet forgiven you because we decided to live in England. But Dad likes you, and you've won over the boys."

She was delighted that her brothers had been able to make it back from overseas for the wedding. She thought they looked dashing in their dress uniforms. There was many a dashing Prime and lovely vampire woman in the hotel ballroom, as well.

She and Matt had returned to Las Vegas for the wedding. Marcus had insisted on catering the reception, making the buffet table a very popular place. The party was a lively affair, full of Cages, Elliots, and many friends of the mortal and supernatural variety. At the moment the band was playing Sting's "Fields of Gold," and Phillipa wanted more than anything to dance with her bondmate.

But before she could suggest it, Pete Martin came up to them. He was grinning, and Matt frowned when he gave her a peck on the cheek.

"You look lovely," Pete told her. He shook Matt's hand. "You're a lucky man, Bridger."

"So I am," Matt answered. "Excuse me a moment, sweetheart."

He stepped away to speak to Mike Bleythin and Cathy, the female werewolf Mike had brought as his guest. She'd found out about Mike's addiction problem, and was happy to see he was holding a bottled water in his hand.

"I'm glad to have you alone for a minute," Phillipa told Pete.

"Really?" He waggled his eyebrows. "Don't tell me that *now* you want to run off with me."

She laughed. "Actually, I wanted to ask you about the cases you were working on the last time I was in town. Any breaks on either of them?" Though she knew how they'd turned out, she was interested in the mortal take on the cases.

"Oh, lord, the woman wants to talk shop on her wedding day." He shook his head. "The killings and the robberies stopped. We're guessing they were related, and that the perps have moved on. We've alerted every other force in the country, so they'll recognize the MO if anything similar starts elsewhere."

"That's all you can do," she commiserated.

He nodded. "There is a funny twist to the case, though it might not be related. About a month after the robberies stopped, a very large sum of money was donated to local charities."

"Really?"

"It amounted to about ninety percent of the take from all the robberies combined. But nobody could prove it was actually the stolen money, so the charities happily accepted the windfall."

"Interesting." She glanced across the room toward Matt. "I mean, that's nice."

A beautiful vampire woman came up and tapped Pete on the shoulder. "Dance with me," Matt's great-grandmother said to the handsome mortal male. Pete perked up at the glorious sight of her, and gladly let her lead him onto the dance floor.

"Would you like to dance with me?" Jason Cage asked, stepping up to Phillipa. She barely recognized him without his wolf companions.

"No," she answered.

"Ah, well. It's always worth a try."

"But I do have a question for you," she said. "I've wondered about something ever since we met in your dressing room."

"Then ask." He smiled expansively. "A bonded female can be denied no request on the day she is formally acknowledged by her new Family. Which translates to wedding day in mortal-speak," he added.

"You lied about something then," she said. "So I didn't trust you at first. I've wondered what you lied about, ever since."

"I'm sorry, but I barely remember the conversation."

She refreshed his memory, and he smiled. "George and Gracie," he said. "I told you that they're mostly malamute, but they are one hundred percent wolf. I didn't like insulting them like that, but people tend to be less nervous around them when I lie about their ancestry."

"I think you should go back to your wolves now," Matt said, coming back to her side. Jason nodded, and disappeared into the crowd. "I'm almost beginning to like that boy," Matt said. "Especially now that he's gone."

Phillipa laughed, and put her arms around his waist. "I just heard something curious," she told her bondmate.

He rested his hand at the base of her spine and tugged her even closer. Warmth spread through her from all the places where they touched.

"Pete told me that all but ten percent of the stolen money was returned," she said.

"Really?"

She looked him in the eye. "Did you keep a cut of the take?"

"Call it a finder's fee," he answered. "How do you think a Guardian gets paid, sweetheart?"

She shook her head, and the band began playing a new song. "Oh, no," she complained, leaning her forehead against Matt's chest. "I specifically told them *not* to play —"

"Queen," he complained.

They held each other and laughed.

"This is where we came in," he said.

"And I think it's about time we left," she said, fire racing through her.

"Your wish is everyone's command on your wedding day. And it will always be mine."

"Except on the rare, high-handed occasion when it isn't," Phillipa said, knowing and loving her man. "Let's go."

As they headed for the door, Matt sang along with the band, "And another one bites the dust."

ABOUT THE AUTHOR

Susan Sizemore is the acclaimed bestselling author of *Master of Darkness, I Hunger for You, I Thirst for You,* and *I Burn for You.* Her novella, "A Touch of Harry," appeared in *The Shadows of Christmas Past,* an anthology coauthored with Christine Feehan.

Susan, who lives in the Midwest, loves vampires, basketball, and hearing from readers.

Visit her website at www.susansizemore .com.

We hope ~~~ ~~~ ~~~ t
book. Other Thorndike, ~~~, and Chivers
Press Large Print books are available at your
library or directly from the publishers.

For information about current and upcoming
titles, please call or write, without obligation,
to:

Publisher
Thorndike Press
295 Kennedy Memorial Drive
Waterville, ME 04901
Tel. (800) 223-1244

or visit our Web site at:

http://gale.cengage.com/thorndike

OR

Chivers Large Print
published by BBC Audiobooks Ltd
St James House, The Square
Lower Bristol Road
Bath BA2 3SB
England
Tel. +44(0) 800 136919
email: bbcaudiobooks@bbc.co.uk
www.bbcaudiobooks.co.uk

All our Large Print titles are designed for easy
reading, and all our books are made to last.